Zombi,
You My Love

Zombi, You My Love

WILLIAM OREM

La Questa
PRESS

Woodside, California

For information address
La Questa Press
211 La Questa Way
Woodside, California 94062

Cover and text design by Kajun Graphics
Front cover painting by V. Hector:
TI FI NAN KIAP POT YOU TÉ POU MOIN PANDAN MOIN MALAD
"The little girl brought tea to me when I was sick."

ISBN 0-9644348-2-2

Library of Congress Catalog Card Number: 98-66969

Grateful acknowledgement is made to the following publications for
permission to reprint previously published stories:

"One Who Waits" (under an earlier title "The Emissary") :
Sulpher River Literary Review, "The Spiritual Exercises": *Willow Springs,*
"Laborers in the Valley of the Lord, 1936": *The Wolf Head Quarterly,*
"Chans" (under an earlier title "Away Down South") was given honorable
mention in *The Missouri Review* Fiction Awards.

THIS BOOK IS FOR LAUREN:

"To do that to birds was why she came."

For helping me to understand Haitian culture and better to reflect the complex atmosphere of the island and its people, indigenous and otherwise, I would like to thank: Bernitte Achille and her family, who shared her childhood in Port-au-Prince with me and the many trials she endured in coming to America; Beverly Shieber, who shared her experience as a missionary in Haiti; Dr. David Fletcher, for help with medical detail; Amy Wilentz's excellent *The Rainy Season: Haiti Since Duvalier;* Karen McCarthy Brown's *Mama Lola: A Vodou Priestess in New York;* and most particularly Elizabeth Vieux, not only for correcting the Creole and discussing her homeland but for telling me the whole world is zombified, ready for the salt that will waken us to life.

On my love I leaned my face,
    all quiet.
There I lost myself,
leaving my cares to fade
among the lilies far away.

John of the Cross

Ki-ki-li-ki, o-ewa!
Papa Ogou, tou piti w yo pare.
Papa Ogou, anraje.

Cock-a-doodle-doo!
Papa Ogou, all your children are ready.
Papa Ogou, enraged.

Vodou song

Contents

Prologue

Laborers in the Valley of the Lord: June, 1936

The old man was finally dead. A moment before, it seemed, he had been breathing: soft, unlabored but unvital breaths, mere motion. The breathing that came at the last stage of life, as the spirit whispered its way in and out of the spent clay, seeking egress. Fr. Julian knew it. He had sat by the dying-bed for several nights, the long heatless, airless twilights on the island, while the sky outside the old man's window faded through turquoise and lavender to the color of an amazing field of tropical flowers. He had watched the progression from the dying-bed with its smell of disinfected sheets and mosquito netting night after night, seeing those flowers spread their silks along the quiet western horizon. On the fourth or fifth night—at this time he was no longer certain how long it had taken—the flowers budded, blossomed, in such an eruption of color that he had gasped, cried out, though whether he made any actual sound would remain unclear. The noise inside his own head had been a single, ecstatic word. Then the triumphal air tensed and faded, quickly, as if bundling its secrets.

The old man had spoken at just that moment. Had he not? Had he not said something to Fr. Julian, raised his head just a fraction off the pelican down pillow they insisted he use, though up until the illness he had remained the most austere of the missionaries? Had he not raised his sallow features, those worn places of skin on bone that had grown to such significance as to seem to hold meaning in each furrowed line beside the ancient mouth or crowded around the vanishing brow? Had the dry mouth itself not, at least, moved—given some faint benediction to accompany Fr. Julian's vision?

He could not say for certain. All he knew was that the old man had died then, at that moment; or at least, when next Fr. Julian became aware of him, he realized that he had already for some time been listening to the strange absence of breathing in the room. It was a stillness that was not a companion to the whispering, fading sounds he had grown used to night by night, but was instead merely the recognition of their having ceased. And there was something suddenly terrible in the realization, something beyond the anticipated. The blankness of breath in that room where the old man had served God for years was not a substitution of the new presence, death, for the old. It was not a replacement of non-being in the hollow vault of being. Rather there was the merest absence in that place, something startlingly small. The silence of the old man was now a fact of equal importance to the steel pole descending from the ceiling to which no fan had ever been attached; the rope baskets that held their simple clothing suspended on wooden rods; the bureau of books and meditations the old man had shipped from America at his own expense. By that tiny amount, the room was something less than it had been. And if this could happen, Fr. Julian feared—if a room could become, by even a small portion, irremediably *less*—could not more be removed? Could not holes be opened up unseen in things, to fester and grow?

So he left the sickbed and drew the partition that served as a door and paced the upper hall of the compound. The others were sleeping—dawn was an hour or more away, and the trees and all the birds in them lay suddenly stilled, as if in anticipation—and he was the oldest one there, the most acclimated to the hard, demanding work of the mission. The others were younger, stronger in body but green, unfleshed in the spirit. They were laborers for the holy office but had yet to be stripped by its demands, like the palm stripped of its skin and the rich bruised life showing within. The natives had shown him once how to draw sustenance from a barrel cactus; bending the crook side-arm of the plant with careful hands, an oil-dark woman had punctured it deftly with her teeth, opening her mouth to show where the plant's fluids squirted out. Fr. Julian knew he was like that now: broken open on all sides, his juices flowed out into the people and the land, and the core, the husk of himself left exposed to sun.

He had ridden back past that spot some time the following month, as they were bringing the host to the poor in St. Marc and discovered a graveyard where Baron crosses had been erected. When the others stopped to pull them down he had remembered the barrel cactus, had looked for it and found it with one withered arm, almost unable to believe it could possibly be the same plant. The split section was brown-gray and lifeless from the place where it had been bitten all the way to the tip.

And now the old man was gone, it was only he, Fr. Julian, who remained. He stood on the little second floor balcony where breakfast would be served and looked into the unspeaking east without sunrise and without stars, and listened to the world painlessly revolve. He was quite alone.

□　□　□

In the morning they canceled the daily medical rounds and devoted the day to a period of prayer, followed by an extended Mass for the dead. There would be a more formal observation later, when time permitted. The new brothers had looked up to the old man as the one most senior in work and elevation, even in the months when he drew away into his room and isolated himself from them all. He had seen his own death coming in the manner of the pale horse, and toward the end he had shirked duties, even failing to appear for the holy bread on his tongue, in favor of remaining at his writings. Fr. Julian had been the only one allowed to go in and see him then, in that long, strange time of his drawing away, which was so odd to the young brothers for whom he had been a figure not merely of distant veneration but a close and palpable love. The old man had moved among them with as much ease as a recruit twenty, thirty years his junior. When recalled by the Archdiocese after the U.S. announced that the occupation would end he had refused, which was unprecedented; and been granted a stay, which was unheard of. The overall effect of his labor on the island was almost above real calculation. Save for Fr. Julian, the mission was his.

Then he had grown distant to the young ones and had taken more and more frequently to his room and his writings. All afternoon long and then deeply into the nights he wrote in his journals. They were not sacred writings, neither studies of scripture nor exegesis, but explication of the work he had done in St. Marc, of the place he had almost forced out of the earth through his own will. Fr. Julian had seen the books. At times the writings moved into, if never bombast, something akin to pride, though some reserved part of him would not accept that the old man was guilty of a sinful self-loving. Like those of a grand architect, his meditations were full of plans for every step of the actions to be taken. He spoke as if the island and its spiritual and political future were peculiarly his, as if it was incumbent upon him to underscore his intentions in ink and in detail before some weaker hand took hold and he was unable any longer to see them enacted.

At other times the tone seemed, to Fr. Julian's eye, to move into justifications of what the old man had done. There was a feeling of uncertainty, a page or five or ten pages that read almost like lament, like only half-formed misgiving for what had been created under the tutelage of his boundless energy. But more frequent were the plans, the constructions, the exhortations to himself and future workers regarding labors not yet accomplished. In time these always swept away the hesitant passages, like a strong hand casting aside doubt. And finally the mere reportage that came in the end, when his mind began its descents: the bland and colorless and ultimately child-like scribbling of names, dates, minutiae. The corners of pages crowded with prayers and meaningless word games, acrostics on the phrases *cos tertium fecit* or *en de nux* followed out obsessively. When the old man became an invalid, Fr. Julian had concealed the books.

The burial took place in the late afternoon, no supplies being available for preservation of the body and the long heat having shown no sign of relenting. So far the temperatures had wilted and destroyed three out of seven rows of corn the brothers had planted in the tilled land out back; had killed four out of seven cattle and almost all the new shade trees. Only three palms and one mapou had survived, the broad stumps of the others found upended in the light, their desiccated root systems crumbling to the hand. Following the old man's last coherently-stated design they had replanted the three palms together at the center of the compound, as a symbol of their faith and determination, allowing for the time when their roots would swim and merge into one.

Clean water supplies were low and the brothers traveled to a watering hole out in the countryside to bathe, a longish trip that required almost as much sweating in the execution as was washed clean by the immersion. But despite the shortage they cleaned the old man's body, Fr. Julian wiping the soft, translucent arms with a towel, the soft muscle under the arms, while a younger recruit wept silently as he dried off the long stretched feet. Fr. Julian saw the recruit going carefully around the wounded place on the left foot where the bone had been broken by a horse's hoof during an early altercation in which the old man had struck a native with a riding crop. He refused treatment and it had caused him to walk oddly thereafter, not to limp, but to carry himself always on that side as if supporting some unseeable burden. The young recruit dabbed at the wound as if fearing the old man might flinch.

There was illness again in the compound and some of the brothers were not fit to labor, but several of the healthy ones dug a hole in the unused burial plot the old man had ordered to be erected within reach of the mission. The earth was resistant and three brothers had to work at it with shovels, finally removing their shirts before the work was done. Having no coffin they wrapped the naked form in cloth and placed the old man directly in the black ground, a small cross of wood in one hand, and covered him over with the hard-crusted soil. It was a burial after the designs of the old man himself, embracing an absolute humility in death, and wise in a land where the clothes in which the dead wasted and the wood in which they slept were so vitally needed for services to the living. The old man had no love of obsequies. He had only been adamant that whites would never cremate their dead as the natives were reported to, because it was against canon law and trumpeted a disbelief in the final resurrection.

Two brothers were reading from scripture over the grave and when they paused there was a time of silence among the gathered. One of the nonclerical workers, a gray-headed half-negro man named T'loko, broke the ceremony by suggesting that Fr. Julian be given the day away from his rounds in order to accommodate his great sorrow. Behind the half-white a small gathering of natives stood, fanning themselves and looking away. Fr. Julian knew that T'loko was eyeing him with challenge, for he had seen that Fr. Julian himself felt no sorrow. The passing of the old man and his realization of that morning under the absolute blackness of the eastern sky had stayed with him like a small piece of the vanishing room. He inspected the hole, examined it, but still found no presence of loss, and thus no sorrow; only the deprivation of the thing, the place inside the room upstairs that had been occupied and now was not. He went that day about his rounds, even riding into St. Marc despite the warnings of fever.

☐   ☐   ☐

In the evening one of the brothers came into his room with a paper-framed lantern that passed a glow onto his features and asked if Fr. Julian needed anything. It was an act of kindness but simultaneously, Fr. Julian felt, of boldness. He raised his hand in a silent gesture and the young brother went away, taking the colored globe with him. Fr. Julian recited his vespers quietly with his eyes averted from the window until the land had fallen into true night, not wanting to see the colors that might emerge or dwell on their meaning. Then there came a quick dusty knock at the curtain ring over his door.

"What will you do?" T'loko asked. He did not bring a lamp with him but stood in the gloom, his gray pomp of hair showing tall and unkempt around the rising dark cranium.

"Wait and see," Fr. Julian said, after a time. "Continue his works."

"Continue his works? *His* works? Or continue the works of Christ?"

"Continue the works of Christ which moved through him," Fr. Julian answered, slowly. "We know not the method, nor the medium, of God's plan."

"God's plan?" T'loko scoffed. "This was not God's plan. This has not been God's plan for years. This, all this around us, the boards on which we stand. This is his plan. *His* plan."

"And you would have known to do it better?" Fr. Julian turned, harsh against the hidden face. "You, who are even now only half-Christ's, you who speak English well but are stranger among us than even the natives? You who have grown spiritually fat on his work, who have been made welcome under his guidance, who have been given the keys to the garden by his hand when your own mother raised you savage? You could have built with your hands such a place?"

"No," T'loko said.

"And could you have arranged to have the trenches dug and lines to catch rainwater and convert it for drinking? And to have not one or two but three operating rooms installed downstairs, even before we have doctors or supplies? And to have started training the natives in converting straws to brick, even before we have teachers for the schools we have yet to build? You could have had that kind of a future vision?"

"No," T'loko said.

"No," Fr. Julian said, reseating himself in the star-cast gloom. "Then what would you...?"

"Burn it," T'loko said. "Burn it to ashes. Burn it for Christ."

Fr. Julian laughed. "And send them where? Send all these hard-working soldiers where? After we have expiated ourselves by purging the land of us. Send them where?"

But the other man was gone. He had come and passed so silently that later, when he had finished reading the last of the books on which the old man had been working, snapped off the light and remembered to cover the battery so it would not corrode in the salty air, Fr. Julian was uncertain as to whether the half-breed had actually spoken to him or merely stood, close-lipped, dividing the doorway with his presence. Outside his little room the far southern constellations moved in their slow unlimited course and Fr. Julian cast his mind among them, saying to the stars: What now? What now?

□ □ □

In the morning he was awakened from a soundless sleep. It was not T'loko this time, the T'loko of reality or the one of his dreams, but the young-faced brother again. He was less presumptuous now without the evening to hide behind, merely a red-cheeked boy whose hair was cropped short up around his ears in a tonsure signifying his status. "It's the body," he said.

Fr. Julian rose and dressed. In a few minutes the face returned, watching as before the floor under Fr. Julian's feet, and unable to say the name. "Please hurry, Father," he said. "Before the others see."

Fr. Julian followed the lantern as the boy carried it swinging out into the dawn light where it was no longer needed, gesturing with it toward the trees as if indicating a general condition of things. "It's there," he said. There was a child's quaver, a high register, in his voice.

"Where?" Fr. Julian said, the morning heat already touching against his skin. "Where?" But the boy could not lead him. He walked in the direction of the mute lamp and away from the compound, away into the quiet trees, behind him now only the sounds of the first wakers stirring from their morning offices. He had slept long; individual prayer would be concluding soon, with matins to follow in the chapel. He walked past the voiceless light and forward until he saw the grave.

The ground had been clawed and scratched open like a wound, the stark blackness of under-soil flung and exposed in brilliant gashes across the harder crust. It looked as if it had been worked at by sharp hands, frantic grabbing motions throwing stone and root in a frenzy to dig deeper. The old man was there, half out of the earth, his naked chest torn and thrashed. He lay only partly consumed in the soil, as if resting.

"I thought... it might be... be a sign," a small voice whispered behind him. The young brother had left the paper-shaded lamp sitting on the earth and come slowly to Fr. Julian's side. "The dogs have been at him all night."

"Dogs," Fr. Julian said. "So it has come to this."

"I thought it might be a sign," the young brother said, and when Fr. Julian looked over at him he saw the wild light of superstition in the eyes. Really they were young for this kind of work; for the world as it was down here. "The natives..."

"The natives are savages," Fr. Julian said. "Their ways are not Christ's ways."

"Yes, Father," the young face assented, seeking the ground.

"Go get the shovels. The others will be at matins for another hour. They will notice our absence but we will make excuses. We have time."

The face, looking glowingly, unbelievingly up at his: "Yes, Father."

"And brother. You will have seen nothing here. Do you understand me? Shut your eyes. There has been nothing here. There is nothing here. There is nothing."

"Yes," the young one said, and was gone. Fr. Julian looked at the tired skin shining once more in the sun like a blossoming pale death flower and he thought to himself: thus it comes to the flesh. Thus and nothing else will it come to all of the flesh.

Thomas

I saw this happen: a middle-aged woman took her laundry to a tidepool near the shore at La Saline. The first thing she did was to make the sign of the cross over the water. Then she dropped the bundle of clothes, somewhat more than most had, on the ground and lifted up her sundress to urinate in the pool. Then she squatted down in the water and rubbed her clothes in it with a white, stonelike piece of hard soap. After she was done she cupped her hands and took a drink. Then she went home.

When I told Ava about that she said it wasn't the worst she'd seen: CARE had sent through a dozen crates full of Swiss cheese in paper wrappers in the summer of 1980 and the villagers all took them out to the water and tried to do their laundry with them. Later on they complained that the American soap did not make very good suds. Also once she had seen a Haitian man come into the mission hospital with a compound fracture jutting up pink out of his leg; he was *Aristide,* from the days when the little priest's followers were vocally racist, and he always swore he would refuse any help from the *blans.* Instead the *bokor* had packed the wound with cow dung and wrapped dirty cloths around it for three days before the man started passing out.

I got on the boat going across the water to Ile de la Gonave and paid the skipper in American money. I always carried some loose coins because the kids would form a tight circle around you as you walked and look into your eyes while underneath the ring of hands, if you let them form the ring, someone's quick fingers were going through any open pocket. Nor could I hide the fact I was an American, not with white skin and the camera strap. But Haiti was different from anywhere I had been before. No one was teaching begging here, the way they did in Belfast and Mexico City and Morocco; Morocco, where there were actual training sessions held once before every tourist season and outside every tourist hotel. The people here did it because they were starving. And they simply didn't believe that a *blan* could go outside without money oozing from the cracks.

Aside from the skipper there were six or seven others with me in the boat, a tar-painted bark that could safely carry about five. It was the same kind of homemade structure that was being used every day now by people who were trying to sail from St. Louis-du-Nord and Cap-Haitien all the way north to the Florida Keys, and were being turned away by American gunships once they got there. Many, according to the Catholic *Radio Soleil*, were diving right in with the sharks and making a swim for it while still several miles offshore.

The people onboard this boat were all Haitians, except for one man who might have been with a health organization but looked more like a head waiter somewhere. He had a tiny moustache that he shaved into a line and weak, sallow skin underneath a straw hat he had picked up from some local vendor. The vendor, whoever it was, had probably seen him coming from about a hundred yards off and known he was about to make the best sale of the week. This fellow was like that.

"*Journaliste?*" he asked. The British accent was apparent even in his French.

"Photos," I said.

"Been down before?"

"Once. A few years back."

"Well, we're all here now," he grinned, his sweating second chin appearing under the smile. His teeth were very exact, as if he clipped them like fingernails. "The French papers, Lord God, it follows they'd be here. Everything's about to blow and they've got a grand guilt complex to assuage by watching it happen. The Italians, the Spanish, they're here too. But the French, Lord God. The other day I came down out of my hotel room—I'm staying at the Holiday Inn—don't you love it? A Holiday Inn, here in the seventh circle of Hades. Ice machines and the whole works. And I came down to breakfast and I met a man covering Namphy for *Le Figaro*. "Figaro, Figaro," he intoned at me, in a sudden baritone voice that caught the attention of the others. "You are with whom?"

"Freelance," I lied. The *Post* had partially sent me and I had partially sent myself but I wasn't feeling the necessity of explaining all that.

"Thank the Lord God. That means you can avoid all the backbiting the rest of us blokes are engaged in. Who gets dinner at the old-money mansions. Who gets the *tap-tap* with the driver who knows the back way." He chuckled; good times at the foreign desk.

"I suppose you're *Guardian?*"

"I should say not," the man bristled, and had to rearrange himself on the seat as the riders jostled against each other. "The *Royal*. On Namphy myself. May write a book. Wait and see."

There was a pause while the Caribbean sun worked its way deeper into our skin, like a burning film. The old-money mansions were all in the capital or Pétionville or Delmas, absurdly extended constructions with twenty bedrooms or staggered, multitiered balcony fronts in the plantation style favored during the occupation years. It was only a boat ride from there to the lesser islands, where the poverty was as bad as anywhere on earth.

"Where in America?" the *Royal* asked.

"Lots of places," I said. "Washington. But I haven't even been there in a while. The work keeps me traveling."

"Yes indeed," he assented, as if we were journeymen who had bonded on this point.

The colors were amazingly bright to look at, and when Ile de la Gonave came into clarity with its distinctive up-and-down rise, a young, rather beautiful woman in the front of the boat went into a trance. Evidently the skipper's daughter, she stretched out backward with her fingers and hair dangling lightly down into the water, leaving long, silky trails. The skipper himself seemed almost unaware of her, though he held firmly to her legs with one hand. The *Royal* caught my eye.

"It's the occult thing," he whispered, though the English made that unnecessary. "Superstition very powerful down here. Very popular. And dramatic too, smashing for the papers. Makes one feel the whole island is imperiled in its soul."

He lifted one hand in a mild histrionic gesture. The wind was in us now and the boat began to move more rapidly, the skipper holding the singing woman's legs under one arm without taking his eyes from the prow. I sat alone for the rest of the trip, thinking about the land and about the peril of the soul.

Zombi, You My Love

On the night Johnny Renelus was turned into a zombi, he hopped out of his coffin, ran to the house where his mother and four sisters lived, and kissed them in their sleep.

"I'm sorry, *manman*," he whispered to the old woman's curled form, awkwardly bent over the side with the missing arm as if she were protecting something. "But I'm so dead now. Ain't no help for it."

In the greenish moonlight he could see the grave-dirt marking their cheeks where his lips had touched.

□ □ □

On the second night he lay out in the uncut grass of the Titanyen graveyard and waited for the *bokor* to make his call. When a dead man is made zombi, the *bokor* can claim him as a personal slave; he will have to do anything the *bokor* wants, for as long as the *bokor* wants it. Some, Johnny knew, had been sent down into the sand mines to labor all night, like tireless mules; some had crossed the border into the D.R. to turn the massive wooden spikes of the sugar mills, in the days before electric machinery. Some were the *bokor's* personal servants: they stayed in his cellar like rats and rose whenever he called them, carrying the *bokor's* horse if it was tired and singing songs from the dead stench of their mouths. Johnny had heard of one night when the *bokor* had friends in his house. In order to amuse them he had one of his zombis hold out its hand and the *bokor* set the thumb on fire with a match. They lit all their cigars from the burning hand and then they sat back and watched the zombi's face as his thumb slowly dripped and blackened. The expression never changed.

Now it was his turn. He had died of malarial fever, *gwo chalè,* and it had taken him too long to wrestle his spirit out of the confines of the flesh. That was his fault. His friends at the woodcutting shop, when they found out he had the *chalè* and was not going to be able to shake it away or live with it, advised him to die quickly.

"Get on out of the skin, man," Ezil Layaren said. "Give it away before *Nwa-nwa* sees you go. You can beat him to it."

The others all nodded agreement. *Nwa-nwa* was the name given to the *bokor* around Les Cayes, although his real name was Rouleau Piti. He called himself *Nwa-nwa* and all the people Johnny knew called him that, and besides, it was bad luck to pronounce the *bokor's* family name even if you knew who he was. The moment you did it you opened up a connection between the *bokor's* name and your own name, like opening a window that would follow you around all day. The *bokor* could look through and see you there, just as if you had called him.

The *bokor* had not liked Johnny Renelus when he was alive. They had not been enemies, but one day the *bokor* walked into the shop when Johnny was working, and out of all the woodcutters, only Johnny had refused to bow his head.

"You know who I am?" the *bokor* asked him.

"Know about you," Johnny said, brushing sawdust from his upper lip where the sweat made it stick. He was just doing his work, not looking up at the *bokor* but not looking away either; he was doing his work.

"Why you don't bow your head, boy?" the *bokor* said. "Why not?"

"Don't see no king of the world in here," Johnny said. He was doing his work and he hadn't meant to make a scene with the *bokor*, only now the *bokor* was confronting him in front of the others and an anger was rising inside Johnny and he knew he wasn't going to back down. The anger was red and thin, like a vein growing inside him, and whenever he felt it he knew he wasn't going to back down, not even to a Macoute. His mother had told him once that this anger was both his fortune and his curse, same as it had been for his father; when Johnny felt it before he had raised his fist to a Macoute man and once to two men with machetes. He did his work.

"We'll see," the *bokor* said.

After he left the woodcutting shop Johnny's friends swore that the *bokor* had cast something at him, just subtly, before walking away. Some said they had seen a quick flick of his hand in Johnny's direction, others that he had raised a finger and marked the air around where Johnny stood with a *point*. Johnny himself had seen nothing. It was not long afterward that he caught the *chalè* that killed him.

So he had tried to die quickly, going home at once to his mother's house when he coughed blood into his hands and knew for certain that the heat and the sweating were not going to stop. He went home to the little house near the water at Les Cayes where he had been born and lay down on the same woven mat and tried to die. But it would not come.

"What you lying down in the middle of the day for?" his sister said. She was walking through on the way to her own job; she had found work a month ago, and the day before her boss had told her and her friends to only come in half-days now because he didn't need *bamma* any more than that. Her boss was a white man from South Africa.

"Trying to die," Johnny said.

"Yeah?"

"Trying," he said.

When his mother heard he was lying on the mat in the middle of the afternoon she at first became angry, believing he had been fired. Then she knelt over and smelled him for tafia.

"You drunk, boy?" she said.

"Trying to die, *manman*," Johnny said without looking up. He was half-curled on the mat and the sweat came down off him in little audible drops. "I got the *chalè* and I got to die fast."

"Oh my baby," his mother said then, her stern broken features softening and the one arm trying to take him in and rock him. "Baron leave my baby be, leave this one be..." But Johnny remained bent halfway on the floor, and all his *manman* could do was to roll him back and forth like a wooden horse on rockers. In a little while he was dead.

□   □   □

On the third night he came out of the coffin again and walked around the colorless grass of the cemetery and listened to the waves landing softly beyond the line of scrub. He wondered that the *bokor* had not come to claim him, wondered how long he would have to wait for the labors to begin. It seemed to him he had been dead a long time now, and the numbness that had begun creeping over him the first night had grown until he felt every part of his body was beginning to disappear: he wondered if he were even still made of physical stuff or if he had passed over already into a spirit-body. He went and kicked his foot lightly against the side of the stone mausoleum where he had been laid by his mother and sisters and a small crowd of people, the sisters whooping loud and his mother resting herself down against the lid of his coffin while the priest threw soil and tried to say something about the future life of the just. But he could not feel anything. His toes seemed numbed and absent; it was only on inspecting them that he found they were still in place. His fingers too were strangely numb and disappearing. He decided he must be vanishing into spirit form bit by bit, like an angle of shadow as the day increases. Perhaps if he waited long enough, Johnny thought, his body would slip out of itself completely and he would be free, rising up above the palms and dappled banyan trees like a clean shaft of moonlight. Then the *bokor* appeared.

He was standing at the gateway to the cemetery, wearing a formal suit and Baron Samedi hat and carrying a cane, his hands luminous inside two white felt gloves. He looked as if he were wearing the fanciest clothes he had, which were not entirely black but a deep shade of gray with pinstripes in the jacket and a slightly wider stripe in the pants. He stood halfway in and halfway out of the cemetery and called out.

"All zombi mine, come on here," the *bokor* said, in a long, sing-song kind of way. "All you zombi made mine, come on here."

Johnny went to him and stood by.

"That the best clothes your family have to bury you in?" the *bokor* asked, flicking grave dirt unhappily from his shirt collar and cuffs. "Well, well. It just have to do."

□　□　□

At the *bokor's* house Johnny was set to work carrying plates and bottles back and forth from the kitchen. The *bokor* was entertaining a large number of guests all the time, and different groups came to see him almost every night. There were people from the army, wearing their olive-green uniform pants and casual shirts thrown over them; one night a man who was called the General came by, drinking heavily and smoking cigars inside the house and laughing. It was not Namphy or Désinor, Johnny knew, because the General was a mulatto and Johnny had seen photographs of these men in the *Haïti Progres* when he had been alive. But the General apparently enjoyed the *bokor's* parties, because he came back several weeks in a row, and always when he was in the room there were people standing around him and laughing loudly when he laughed. The General drank constantly and sometimes he shifted his fat belly in the chair where he always sat, sliding his pistol around underneath the belt so it would not stab him.

"More clairin, *zizi*," the *bokor* said to Johnny, calling him by his zombi name, the name that held power over his soulless body. Johnny brought clairin and tafia for the General, and the General would laugh whenever he saw Johnny and take the bottle from him and toast the *bokor*. Sometimes the parties went until nearly dawn.

When the party was over the *bokor* would sigh and tell him to clean up the mess the General always left behind, and later he would come into the kitchen and complain about the food, saying how zombi could not cook. Then he would put a spoonful of sugar on Johnny's tongue and light a match and blow it out and send Johnny to the shed out back where the zombis stayed.

□   □   □

Johnny did not know for how long he had been a slave to the *bokor*, because since he died he had no sense of time. But the moon had risen thin and sparse more than once outside the leaning shed, and it was voluptuous fat again along the mountains on the night when he first saw the *bokor's* girl. The General was back and had given the *bokor* a present of a human ear in a box, and the *bokor's* expression when he opened it made the General laugh until tears appeared on his heavy cheeks. The *bokor* took the box then and smilingly put it aside, nodding to show it was all right, the General could have his fun; but later Johnny had seen the *bokor* frantically washing his hands, his expression drawn. Johnny was carrying empty glasses into the kitchen and there she was, the *bokor's* girl, hollowing meat out of a boiled lobster. She looked up as he came in.

Johnny set the glasses down so they would make no noise. She had a thin, even face that reminded him of sea-turned wood: a large clean forehead shone out underneath her hair-wrap, and her eyes that had first met him when he came into the room now danced in little trills of energy around the lobster meat half-emptied onto a plate. She would not look up.

"You so beautiful," Johnny said. It was the first time he had spoken since his zombification.

"Don't touch me," the girl said, her thin hands going back behind her head once to pull the hair-wrap straight and then working more quickly. "I'm dead."

□   □   □

After that he began seeing her more and more around the *bokor's* house. She passed him when he was bringing charcoal into the kitchen and her seeing eyes looked at his and away. When the *bokor* made him clean out the gutters he spotted her in the distance, coming across the treelined fields with a basket of bright mangoes balanced on her head. One evening when the *bokor* sent him back to his shed Johnny found a yellow piece of paper there with a word written on it in crude strokes of pencil: *M'ionet*. He folded it into a knot and worked it between two boards.

People continued to come by for the *bokor's* evening parties and sit on the front veranda drinking or smoking cigarettes with cocaine powdered on them. When the *bokor* had become a little drunk himself and was smiling steadily from his wicker chair, he would say that some evening he was going to show them his *clair lune,* a little moon he had caught in a mirror and could hold now in his hands. When he wanted to the *bokor* could speak in schoolbook French, an effect that was startling. Always the guests wanted to know what was this little moon; some remained quiet, as if leery of being taken in, while others flattered the *bokor* by saying his powers were surely enough to do such a thing. When they flattered him the *bokor* called for more rum and more cocaine, and fireworks, and seemed very pleased with himself; but the evening would end and he would always say no, his *clair lune* had to remain his alone for now. But perhaps they would please him by coming again?

Then one night the General started teasing the *bokor,* saying how there was no moon kept in a glass; and when the *bokor* politely assured the company that there was, the General only laughed louder, as if the two of them were in on an unannounced joke. When the General laughed the fat rim of his neck jumped in and out around his collar. The *bokor* tried to dismiss the subject and ordered more drinks but the General teased him again, and by the end of the evening Johnny could tell the *bokor* had made himself very drunk. When the first group stood up to leave at dawn the *bokor* suddenly clapped his hands and commanded them to all sit down.

"*Zuzu,*" he called. "*Zuzu.*"

She appeared from the kitchen in a white dress and hoop earrings. Johnny was amazed to see his zombi girl in clothes like a living woman: her bandanna was gone and her hair opened freely out to the night air, framing the lean narrow face, skin the color of sand after water has caressed it. Slowly she came walking forward until she was full in their midst.

As the men watched, M'ionet began to dance, her legs coming slow and powerful from the edge of her dress and carrying her forward minutely or straight up, up sometimes on the fronts of her bare feet, the pale bottoms of her feet showing, so that Johnny thought in another step she would lift herself into the air and be gone. Then she descended, poured down into the earth with her spine bent low like something flowing, a weird, rhythmless pulsation of movement touching off movement. Around them all she danced, the men on the veranda and the ones standing or crouching in the dry grass, and where there had been sounds of talking and even argument there was now only silence, silence and the little winking eyes of the men's cigarettes in the dark. It was so quiet that after a minute Johnny realized he could hear bugs clicking inside the paper lanterns.

Then she finished her dance and there was a roar of men clapping their hands and calling for *anko, encore*. The *bokor's* eyes shone wetly in the candles.

As she walked back into the house the guests all tried to look into her face, but her face had the lifeless quiet again that is the look of a zombi. The General alone stood up from his chair, but the *bokor* interceded.

"Not this one," he said, taking the General's hand by the wrist. The General looked down at the hand touching his own as if it were a parasite. "This one is special," the *bokor* said, coughing a little. And he sent her away.

□　□　□

In the weeks afterward, Johnny spoke with M'ionet again in the kitchen. He told her that he too was dead and that she had nothing to fear from him. He touched the calloused edges of her fingers with his own and once his hand found its way to the smooth forehead and gently down to where it met the small bridge of her nose. M'ionet continued to work but when he touched her she closed her eyelids and let him feel across her skin.

Still she was afraid the *bokor* would hear; always her eyes flashed toward the half-swung doors when they met. Her mother had refused to dance with the *bokor* at a hill ceremony for Kouzinn Zaka, to which the *bokor* had only replied, "We will see." That very day she had stepped on a nail on the way home and gotten tetanus and died. She slipped the shoe from her foot and showed him the little bite-kiss where the tip had entered. Now she slept every night in the *bokor's* room, and even in his bed, although the *bokor* never touched her. Each night he sat on the side of his mattress and looked at her for a long time, drinking until his head sagged while she danced, slowly, slowly; then he commanded her to undress and get into bed. But when she did he only lay next to her with his arms rigid, staring at the gradual turn of the ceiling fan and sometimes groaning. One night she had moved a little in the bed and when her elbow touched his the *bokor* shuddered and left the room.

When the moon was eaten thin and sparse again over the hills Johnny took the yellow paper he had kept and passed it back into her hand. On it he had written *Zombi, you my love.*

The next day the *bokor* brought him into the house and told him there was going to be another party. The *bokor* did not seem pleased with this information; and after he had said it and explained the work that Johnny would need to do in preparation, he stood apart and seemed to think to himself for a while. Johnny thought the *bokor* seemed lonely.

"Well. No use talking to dead man, anyway," the *bokor* said, and sent him out to chop wood.

□　□　□

The party was larger than the ones he had seen so far. A line of cars and jeeps with tinted windows formed gradually in front of the two-story house, and the drinking began before the sun had even gone down. Johnny was up and down from the wine cellar and the iceboxes without cease, taking bottles into the kitchen and carrying plates of food out onto tables. There were more men in the olive-green costumes of the army, but this time they had taken care to wear matching shirts and pants and to have their shirts tucked in. There were also men he had never seen before who wore gray, a white man who came with bodyguards and who smoked a pipe made out of a hollow tube of dried corn, and even some who openly wore the red bandannas of the Macoute. No one noticed him as he worked.

Eventually the General showed up, arriving in a jeep with a small red and green flag pushed down into the antenna slot. He was wearing his army uniform and there were medals on the left side of his jacket. Johnny put out his hands to take the jacket but the General ignored him and walked to the middle of the room. He was not laughing tonight.

At twilight the *bokor* appeared, walking among the guests in a colored sash and loose-fitting shirt that he only wore for ceremonial occasions. He had a bright earring in one ear and had bathed and shaved himself. He walked from table to table with a wide, friendly smile and asked how different people were doing, who would care for more *pistaches*, had they tried the cheese. Even the slight round of his belly seemed pleasant. When the General sat down in the *bokor's* own wicker chair the *bokor* seemed to consider him for a moment and then, managing a smile, went to a different side of the room.

After a while the *bokor* clapped his hands and three young men carrying guitars came in. The small crowd that had formed around the punch bowls moved aside and gave them a center-space. The *bokor* grinned at the room as a whole, and then at the General, who did not smile back. There were men in gray standing around the General now in the *bokor's* chair, and they did not smile either. The guitarists sang *Haïti Chéri* and then started to play a merengue tune that had been popular the year before, and some of the people who had been drinking the most tried to dance with their women. Halfway through the second piece the General clapped his own hands. The music stopped.

"M'ionet," he said.

From behind one of the punch bowls the *bokor* nodded a little, the wide grin staying on his face before and after like a pinned-on thing.

"M'ionet," the General said again, and he did not smile and the men around him did not smile.

"Well, well. The dead ought to be buried," the *bokor* mused pleasantly, as if this were an observation that might be applied to any number of situations. "Don't you agree? My little moon was lovely, *wi,* but my moon has faded away."

He raised his shoulders slightly to the crowd as if to say: No help for it. The General waited in the wicker chair, not speaking. He was wearing mirrored sunglasses and had not taken them off.

"Give me M'ionet, Rouleau Piti," he said slowly. "*Nwa-nwa Piti. Rouleau Piti.*"

The *bokor* tried to laugh a second time, but the sound that came from him was too high-pitched, a little dying cough. The guitarists were beginning to look uncomfortable.

"Please," the *bokor* said to the room, his arms raised slightly in the robe as if he were preparing for a small oration. "We must of course bury the dead... wouldn't you agree? It is only right space..." His second chin shone wet.

Two of the gray-shirted ones who had come before the General moved in behind the *bokor,* who had been leaning toward the doorway to the veranda. "Please..." the *bokor* said feebly, his undrunk eyes going red now around the edges. "Please..."

Johnny stepped out into the center of the room.

"Why don't you bow your head when the *bokor* right there?" he said to the General. "Why don't you bow it, boy?"

The combined faces of the room turned toward him in a slow rush, like the mounting pressure of an overflowing well. The General's expression dropped into a visible slackness even underneath the sunglasses. His mouth hung a little bit.

"What..." he stumbled. "Who..."

"I said, why don't you bow it? Bow down for the *bokor* like you should!"

The man with the corn-stem pipe, who had been watching both the General and the *bokor* from his side of the room, suddenly spread his lips wide and laughed. The General looked as if he had been dealt a physical blow and his entire body began to tremble.

"I'll... have... that... *girl!*" he raged, beating the weak arm of the chair and half-rising. But it was a mistake: the effect was childish and, in an indecisive moment, he allowed himself to fall back again into the seat. Johnny turned toward the crowd.

"Don't see no king of the world in here," he said.

This time the laughter was spontaneous at all tables, and as the General stormed to his feet the *bokor* made a sudden run for the veranda. Eyes turned in that direction and Johnny flew through the back door instead, flew through the kitchen and out the back porch even as he heard things inside beginning to shatter: flew because he was spirit now and no longer needed legs nor feet nor earth underneath to give him passage; he was passage itself. He flew past the edge of the *bokor's* property where no zombi can pass, and passed it; flew past the mapou tree where no spell of the *bokor's* can be broken, and broke it; flew past scrub cactus and underneath crisp spinning stars until he found himself back at the cemetery, three miles or more from the *bokor's* place, dancing around the mausoleums and the boxes and the still unspeaking earth. He pulled coffins from their shelves and checked their gummy remains: he knocked lead-lined doors with his fists until they rang like bells: he hallooed into the ground and slapped it with his hands and listened. And when he found the patch of new black loam that had been broken and turned he grabbed out a spade from a pile and dug deep, deep and straight down and with a zombi's unfailing energy, dug until he had found her and popped the ridiculous lid and pulled his love streaming back out of the earth. The night filled in the hole behind them, and the holes left by his enormous feet as he ran; his feet that were becoming more solid and massy with every step, every step ripping free a grave, until the earth on which he trod shook and had to recognize him.

"You feel it right here," Johnny said, his new arms tense and strong under M'ionet's weightless weight. It was the red vein swimming inside him: the vein that started somewhere in his center and moved itself all the way into his fiery throat and his flying head. "That's the anger in me all along," Johnny sang as he ran. "I guess *manman* was right. I just couldn't put it down."

Chans

In Lapier only two people had buses, Henri Santil and Raymon Ame, and since there was no fixed schedule they competed with each other every day to take riders west into St. Marc. Whoever left Lapier earlier would get to the fish catches first and would be the one with the most riders. Soon the drivers had pushed the departure time back to before dawn, and eventually they were going so early I was told you might want to stay up from the night before and wait out in the dry brush to hear the bus when it went by.

The morning I went to see Ava at the infirmary I waited outside and listened for the bus. In Haiti I never heard birds singing: instead there was an immense quiet that draped the bald-headed mountains, a quietness like a dull weight. I asked a Swiss naturalist about it once and he said there were blue heron and flamingos but no songbirds anywhere on the island, but because of the language barrier it was hard to tell if he was joking. That morning I stood and squatted some in the midst of the great quiet and when the bus drove past it wasn't hard to tell at all.

The *Rose Selavy* was Henri Santil's bus, its name—a Creole pun on *L'eros c'est la vie*—painted across one side in bold white strokes. Santil had taken a series of wooden pews out of an abandoned church somewhere and roped them to the top to make more room. Such roof-riding was not uncommon in the countryside; on an especially good day the riders would be so crammed together that the people in the middle had to trust to the ones on either side not to let go.

"*Je vois c'est bondé chez vous aujord'hui*," I said to Santil when I got inside. "Today you win the game and get all the riders."

"Ame gives his whole business to me today," he said. "No problem with Ame." He was smiling a little bit.

"Why does he do that? Is Raymon Ame ill?"

"*Li pa malad-non*. But he gives all his business to me. Yesterday he told me it was so. He said to me, Henri Santil, tomorrow you will have all my riders. *Comme ça*. Just like this." He showed me the rubbing-together fingers gesture that meant *bon chans*, good luck had come to him.

I liked Henri Santil; he was a stalky, good-looking man who spoke French and aspired to English, an aspiration that made any American his immediate friend. He had surprising blue eyes and wore collared shirts always, even when he was not driving. I couldn't tell quite what had happened to bring him his *bon chans*, but just to be friendly I asked if he thought Raymon Ame should give him all his business every day and he said that would be a pretty good idea.

Down the center aisle there were three riders to a seat and about a foot and a half of room to stand. We drove through the anonymous morning, passing the shapes of people who were out wandering the roads in the predawn gloom. Most of the poor I had seen outside of the capital didn't have enough room to fit more than two or three on the bananamat inside their houses, and in many places they slept standing, *dòmi kanpe*, leaned up against each other to conserve space. Everyone slept in shifts and someone was always out walking for an hour or two before going back. The roads were busy all night with moving human forms.

□   □   □

I found a seat in the mission foyer, looking out at the tumbled hills and scrub foliage that surrounded the building in the midst of a wakening sky. There were a few other people there already, including a young man who was sitting in a foldout chair in the corner. He had a broad clean face and a small ring that he wore on the first knuckle, either because it didn't fit or because he wanted to show it off. He kept looking up at what I took to be a family who were all sitting on the floor on the other side of the room. They looked like a family. The mother had a cloth over her head and was rocking fluidly back and forth, repeating something in a sub-audible monotone. A tired girl leaned against her back, so close they were almost a unit; some younger ones skittered around the front room, inspecting the glass case with the big brass crucifix, the rubber oxygen pump, the pamphlets on safe sex so absurd in a country of rampant illiteracy. Every so often the man in the corner chair would look over at them and grin a hard yellowish grin and he would grin at me also, and nod his head and then look away.

When she didn't appear after a few minutes I wrote a note: *Thanks For All Your Many Thoughtful Efforts Love God.*

The girl at the front desk was named Lamesi Brave. She was a short, efficacious person without much sense of humor, but then she spoke no English and my French was only average. She said she would take the note back but that Nurse Ueding had been with a patient the last time she saw her and might still be busy. She pronounced Ava's name *"you wedding."*

No answer came back, and I started to think that might have been mean. After a little wait I asked Lamesi to take another note.

The second slip read:

You And I Are Like Catherine and Lt. Henry In A Farewell to Arms. She Is A Nurse and He Is In Love With Her.

Then I tore off the last line and wrote a different one in the corner so it read:

She Is A Nurse And He Doesn't Know What He Is.

I told Lamesi to please take this note back to Miss Barkley. She looked upset at that and said there was no Miss Barkley on the staff, so I conceded that the *belle infirmière américaine* would do. It seemed like a long time I was there by the windows not listening to it and eventually Ava came out.

"Thomas," she said, with the wonderful stress she always put on the second syllable. "Is today one of our dates?"

She was beautiful in the Germanic way: blonde hair that would have shone in a tropical sun, perpetually back in a tight knot with a net around it. No makeup around her eyes, which was a good thing, and that poetic neck stuck in a terribly stiff hospital collar. But Ava looked good in her whites.

"Today is our date," I said. If there had been any magazines I would have been leafing one. "I hope you didn't forget. I came a long way."

"You came a long way because it's about to be a civil war," she said. "Don't flatter me, *jounalis.*"

"I'm a *jounalis* who would love to be covering the Bahamas right now."

She smiled at that. "I haven't read *Farewell to Arms.* Isn't that Hemingway?"

"Faulkner. Hemingway did the screenplay later."

"Sometimes I don't know whether you are joking or not, *monsieur.* Oh, yes I do. You are always teasing me. My grandmother used to say *Witz versteckt eine Traurigkeit.* Joking hides a sadness."

I didn't have any answer for that.

"Well then, where were we supposed to go?" she said. "I've already shown you the docks, and the American bar and the painters and the fish markets. And that crazy man selling ices with liquor. I won't touch it and I'd advise you not to either."

"You've started an abstinence committee."

"No. I meant the ice. It sits right out on the ground. And *he* sits on it when no one's buying."

I was looking at her the way I would have looked at any woman back in the States, but Ava wasn't like that at all. There was something hard inside her, harder than anything I had. If things got bad, she had her belief in God—a gritty-toothed version of the tough-love deity they teach in Jesuit schools. Her God would let you get flayed alive by Romans while he sat back calmly and wrote down every crisis of faith you experienced.

"I have a better plan now," I said. "About three degrees north of here is a house on a little plot of land that used to belong to Mister Hemingway for real. It's open to the public and all the cats have six toes. If you want, we could go see."

"Six-toed cats?" Ava said, her expression going blank. "What's wrong with them?"

"There's nothing wrong with them. I think that must be the nurse in you talking."

"Oh. I suppose it is," she answered, and laughed a little at herself. But the laugh was melting, like the block of ice where the vendor crouched selling liquors in sunlight. She sat with me and the grinning man in the chair grinned at her too.

"I can't stay with you for very long today, Thomas," she said. "I'm sorry. We can walk around the compound maybe. But things are... difficult right now."

"Things? Is there…" She stood up by way of answer and I followed her.

The inner spaces of the infirmary smelled sweetly of iodine and chemical disinfectants; there were not distinct rooms so much as cots with sheet walls separating them from each other, some of the sheets hung from bamboo poles. A doctor holding his scrubbed arms up so as to not touch anything motioned me back from the main area and I moved over by a man sitting entirely on a steel-topped table with no pants on. He had an open wound in his thigh and was cleaning dirt out of it with a pencil-tip. Beside him a young woman coughed a gray and rose-colored fluid every few minutes into a cup. The air was hot and thin.

"It's the son of one of the families who live in the village," Ava said. She leaned up against a wall by a bed with the sheets drawn completely around it, like a canopy for an ailing king. "He was out walking in the dark when the bus from Borel hit him. There's concussion and swelling on both sides of his head. We tried to help but he was so malnourished his body just can't fight something like this. Now all we can do is wait. And pray."

"Which bus was it?" I said. "Was it Henri Santil?"

"No," she said. "No, the other one. He's been waiting out front all morning, like a vulture, waiting to hear the verdict. I couldn't explain what was going on with him sitting right there. I wonder how I can even stand to look at him."

"If it was an accident..."

"Oh, Thomas," she said, as if I were the most naive person on the island, which I thought perhaps I was. "He isn't waiting there out of kindness. They say if you know you are going to have an accident it's better to try and kill the person you hit, because otherwise you'll have to pay the hospital bills. He's waiting to see if he has *chans*. If he gets lucky."

She went and washed her arms up to the elbow in a metal sink, her torso leaning prettily inside the white coat; I found myself noticing its curve, the simple beauty of the thing. Out in the foyer the luckless Raymon Ame sat, unbothered by the presence of the family whose son had committed the crime of being a liability if he lived. Through the windows behind him the sun had finally crested the hills in that way beautiful things have of happening in the midst of all human hurt, as if the world were delirious beyond reach in its own joy of coming into being.

"Come outside with me," I said. "Just for a minute."

She seemed to think about it.

"All right," she said.

We went out back and around to the gardens where it was just the big hills rolling up over scrub pines and cactus and a brilliant tide of blue aster flowers. Ava had nothing to say and then after a while she seemed to tremble, neither with weakness nor with anger. She leaned up against me not looking at me and we were quiet, not the overwhelming quiet of the island but the small quiet of two people, for what seemed like a very long time.

After the Rain

After the rain the rivers broke into twos and threes, creating smaller paths that flowed in expanding and unblocked courses along the edges of rice fields and cracked-looking sugarcane fields and across the visible root systems of banyan trees. By evening the water would have dissipated entirely, having been transformed into the full, almost palpable sheets of mist that hung like spirits over the land, drawn out by the unceasing pulse-heat of the sun. But for an hour it came down unimpeded from the scarred hills and across what had been dirt walkways, bringing small drifts of pebble and dead wood; and the loosened earth colored the spilled water a deep rust-crimson so that it was impossible to see it and not think of blood.

The cart was stalled along the side of what had been a dirt path traveling north, parallel to Route Nationale #1. Until the noon flooding blocked its progress, it had been pulled by a team of worn-looking burros with brown, hairless skin that appeared to have been cut for animals of a slightly larger size. They were motionless now, tethered to the shedding boles of twin palms, with that immediate and incredible lack of concern of which only beasts that labor are capable. Under the speckled light their shabby tails swung lazily out and back, trailing bright green horseflies. Half an hour after the rain it was already too hot for the animals to move without being beaten.

"Do you have clean water?" the American man asked. The woman next to him was a missionary and a teacher who had once held part of a stabbed man's lower intestine in her unwashed hands to keep it from spilling out; at another time she had crawled through the glassless window of a small church in Petit Trou-de-Nippes and lay on the blistering roof tiles while Macoute had gone through and shot everyone else inside. She had long ago lost any feeling for God, either belief or skepticism, but remained in her position out of a sense of terrible if irremediable lethargy. It was a lethargy, she knew, larger than any one place or devotion, and it drove her at times to excesses of charitable action. She now held her knees up and a little in between her hands. An observer who did not know her and the way she had lived for the past several years would have thought her squeamish, hesitant to let her legs touch too much of the earwig-filled hay on which they sat.

"No," she said.

"I left what I had back at Port-au-Prince," he said, pronouncing the "t" in the mistaken way of foreigners, "when I packed my things in. Damn it. You didn't bring any at all?"

"No," she said again, and then seemed to examine the word in front of her as if it had weight. "The mission has water."

"I suppose we could just take theirs," the man said, meaning the two Haitian women who owned the cart and who were eating lunch a ways off in a dry patch of higher grass. "That's what we Americans do, right? Come down here and take things away from these people?"

"Moi, je suis canadienne," the woman said. But the man made a gesture with his lips suggesting that this was a foolish distinction.

"What about this stream water?"

"It's the soil runoff that makes it look that way. It's happening all over the island. Deforestation."

"No, I mean, for drinking." The man wiped his wide, sweating baldness with the sleeve portion of one arm. As the last of the rain spattered down on the roofless cart, he had felt comical. But now it was only hotter than before, it seemed, as if the etched silver sun were holding a grudge against its absolute law having been even briefly contravened. "Can we drink it?"

"No."

"No. Just no. You don't have any pills or anything."

"Not like that. The mission..."

"The mission has some," he completed, waving her down. "Miraculous things: little white pills of which the major pharmaceutical characteristic is that we have none. Pretty damn ironic, isn't it? Surrounded by water and dying of thirst?"

The bloody course bubbled across the path in front of them in several places, laying the grass flat directly next to patches that stood parched and unrelieved with tiny black insects crawling across their gnawed lines. For an hour at least they had managed to splash through the gradually deepening tide, the wheels tricking and turning into ruts that were forming around them even as they fell, and the burros splashing unhappily into the thickening mud. Once when the man thought there was no way through the two Haitians had piled up a series of stones for the burros to look at; that had convinced the animals that the ground was still there and had kept them walking, for a bit. But now even that was impossible.

"You could try it without the pills. Only I wouldn't advise that. You're green."

"Green?" he bristled, the lip of fat that protruded from his tight collar showing more as he frowned. "What do you mean by that? Green?"

The woman waited a moment, looking with her odd, vaguely disbelieving expression into the blank air in front of her where the man was not standing before replying. "Well. How long have you been in country? We didn't get the word someone was coming until just this month."

"I came straight to the capital from Miami Beach. But I don't see..."

"Miami!" she cried lightly, and it was difficult for the man to know if he were being laughed at or if the exclamation were something more on the order of joy. She certainly seemed happy enough, he thought, as if she were suddenly charmed at the memory that there had ever been such a place in the world as Florida. "There's a *mambo* who lives somewhere in the Keys; all the locals talk about her as if she were a kind of sibyl. She had to leave because of some scandal, and now she's keeping an eye on everyone." The woman tapped the clean space above her eyes. "You know. In a mystic way."

The man was a little baffled by her response. "I suppose I seem quite the greenhorn," he said, "to someone of your... extensive learning."

"No," she answered without bristling, and he felt immediately dismissed. His sudden petulance at their situation sounded small, even in his own gut. "But your stomach is a greenhorn. That water is full of rotten wood pulp and dead earth. Probably some animal carcasses somewhere upstream too. It doesn't rain around here for weeks, in some places for years, and then when it does everything comes down. Have you had salmonella before?"

"No. Have you?"

"Oh, yes," she said without heat, and again his challenge fell flat. "When you've had it once it's easier to get through again."

He had gotten all his shots, along with two other State Department members, at a little cool doctor's office in Miami, including one for a sexually transmitted parasite of which he wan't even aware. Just before his appointment he had been drinking margaritas at an Everglades-themed bar called *Le Place* and had wondered if the alcohol, about which he lied to the doctors, might somehow counteract the protections. But he didn't say anything to this woman now because he knew somehow that she would only laugh again; laugh not at him, never at him, but merely at the fact of him, come down here to the island with his unburned skin and his body so soft and doughy the beggars outside the airport had wanted to touch him to see if such excess could be real. He had come down to check on the status of three American missions and, in a more vague way, the political implication of their work. People up north were once again feeling uncomfortable about this funny little nation-state. And missions had gone socialist before; even Catholic ones.

Two of the missions he was looking for, he had since learned, were in fact no longer in existence, their hollow and corrupted shells being used as communal living spaces—in one case, apparently at the behest of the liberation-theology priests who had abandoned them. He was traveling to the third outpost of progress now, which was alive and well and had sent the woman to fetch him from the capital, on a ride that was not to have taken more than an hour before the rain came through. The woman had suggested taking the trip by cart, which apparently was a not-unheard-of method of get-around in a country with few and poor roads. Magnanimous, he acceded.

And then there was the woman herself. He had first seen her waiting for him outside the Oloffson hotel, just standing there in the street as if she could stand for another hour or ten hours or ten days if she wanted to, and who didn't seem to need to drink; who didn't seem unsettled in the least by the taxi drivers and beggars who called out to her, their skin so unclean that portions of it were flaking away in little clots; who didn't seem bothered by the sunlight that had been like a hammer on one side of his skull since before he had debarked the little lime-green airplane with its cannon-and-drum insignia. The truth was he had drunk plenty that morning before she came and then had something alcoholic to drink once again while trying to make small talk with her at the bar. But the water had vanished away inside him, almost as soon as his lips touched it. It was her lack of any needs that made him feel small, disappearingly tiny in this insignificant island world. He was State Department. The immense sun was grinding him down like a gnat.

"How long before this flooding drops?" he asked again, hoping at least she would show some irritation at the question repeated.

"Could be another hour," she said. "Maybe more."

"Hey, there," he called to the two women sitting in the dry grass. "Aren't you almost ready to start again? I think the water is down."

"Get Manman-W," one of the women said. The other woman laughed.

"Do you know what she said?" he asked.

"No," the woman lied.

The man got out of the cart and walked a little ways forward on the road. As he passed by the two burros eyed him with small indifference.

Up by the blocked section of path the crimson water was gurgling over the thatch and cactus fields now, smoothing several yard-wide stretches of elephant grass in long, hairlike bunches. Even without careful inspection he could see its level was still on the rise. As he watched, a turtle extended a gray-green neck from under the grass and slipped down again.

The man stood by the edge of the passable road and cursed. The more he thought about it the more heat mounted into his cheeks from underneath the carefully-trimmed line of beard. His beard was his pride; he had not been able to give it a good clip since he had landed, and every day the growing disorder of it irritated him more. The first morning when he awoke in his hotel there had been ants in it, the kind that bite. He passed his hand over his jaw now in a smoothing motion, but the unkempt hair spurted again from under his fingers. He cursed.

"Give me some of that water," he said to the women seated in the high grass. "I'm dying."

They looked at him quizzically, one returning to what she had been doing before when he spoke again.

"Your water. Give me some of it. I represent the American Embassy and I demand you give me some of your water." He reached for the container. At once the two women started chattering at him like birds, making swinging motions with their arms and slapping at his ankles as if to drive him off.

"Give it here! Damn it all! Damn it!"

One of the women grabbed at his wrist and he pushed her down into the elephant grass and began striking her. He struck with his open hand at her face and at her hands, and when she stopped struggling against him he took three steps back and drank enormously from the water, letting it run on his beard. Then he capped it and dropped it back on the grass where he stood and walked back to the cart.

"It's warm," he said to no one, wiping his hand across the red growth at his neck. "Warm and probably full of piss." He was not looking at the woman in the cart, who had not moved from her position during the altercation. The man stood for a minute not looking at her, and then he walked a little way off and came back with a thin, sharp-edged strip of palm bark.

"Permission to get the burros going," he said to no one.

"All right," the woman in the cart said. Her face seemed a

little sad. The man unhooked one of the animals, and walking it a few yards closer so that the women sitting in the grass could see, began flogging it with the strip. At first the animal did not react and the man began to beat it harder, his face growing sweaty and pinched around the nose. By the third and fourth blow the animal had begun to feel the pain, and eventually its white eyes rolled strangely in its head as if looking across the long canopy of trees for some understanding.

Bright Angel

He said he loved her *vraiment;* that seemed the important thing. Miguel Jeanfils was a tall, smoothly-boned boy with kind hands and mouth, a sense of humor that was keen and floated just around his handsome lips. To Fia he appeared to shine, to be full of an unpredictable light; always she was a little foolish when she was with him, a little unlike herself. Her friends commented on it, calling Miguel the "bright angel" because of his noticeably light skin, and Fia the "little *fleu*." But she didn't care. Also his family was rich, by the standards of Port-de-Paix. Miguel had an uncle or a stepfather in politics, he was one day going to be on the cabinet of the president. The uncle or stepfather flew back and forth to Washington, and there were family members in not only Washington but Long Island and *Nuo Yok;* Miguel had been there. Miguel had a life ahead of him.

Then she saw him one night dancing with a fat girl at a local dance. She dropped the basket she had forgotten earlier at the tidal pool off her head and went in to confront him right there, but before she could say anything Miguel turned and saw her, and the old not-herself, not-Fia returned, and she fled the room. She had seen him looking at the other girl, who had big hips and thighs stuffed into an ugly yellow print dress, with the same light and almost-joking face he had for her, and suddenly she could not speak.

Miguel found her outside squatting by the scattered clothes. They talked for a long time and once he started to light a *Comme Il Faut* and then didn't do it, which she took to be out of consideration for her bad lungs. Finally they walked together into a deep field where the sawgrass was as tall as her knees in places and the bougainvillea parted to reveal an oval, whispering place away from the earth, with the little dance hall burning its lights in the distance, and the blankness she was walking into seemed to her to be made of him, of Miguel, as if he were weaving it around and around her like a tent. His arm grew stronger across her shoulders.

And now Miguel was gone, as if that night outside the earth had never happened. But he had left his mark in her body: he had printed her with himself like placing his hand down in the soft clay-sand by the water. She felt the new life stirring and hurrying inside her, although it was only a month and a week old, felt the change in her body and the imprinted mark on the sand that would not wash away. And Miguel was gone.

All day she walked with her hands there, pretty hands, she thought; slim hands and slim fingers, not worked up into roughness the way her brother's were from swinging machetes up in the hills, or her father's from working for years in the sand mines. Often now her father had no work, and at those times he sat at a foldout table in front of the house and did nothing. If she passed him in this condition he would invariably call to her to come look at his palms, hold the puckered scarred flesh up to her like a justification. Always she was careful about the appearance of her hands, since the *femme sage* had told her that *hands will catch the man*. That was where she should have gone now, she knew, with her troubles; but the *femme sage* had been peeing blood and would see no one.

Now she walked back and forth from the market stalls where she alone had work, and back again home, every day, with her slim pretty fingers cupped and holding the secret life she knew was hidden just inside her stomach. Miguel, she had heard, was in the D.R. for a while with his people. His own light complexion showed where his roots lay, in the old aristocracy; and there were stories told about how the D.R. boys came over only to use Haitian women, how they felt a dark-skinned woman was only good for one thing. When she saw them, her friends, not knowing the quick secret mark that was in her, teased her about her bright angel. Fia had never believed their stories, but now she had her doubts.

□　□　□

On the night she decided to see the *houngan* a town-wide shutdown was imposed. Macoute came through and knocked over the banana carts and shot holes in the orange carts where she had been working only moments before. A young woman whom she knew, Ane Baptiste, was standing by the carts and one of the men grabbed her by the arm and made her dance with him. Several of the Macoute were drinking.

Fia left the market by the back way and walked quickly through the dusty streets, where people were pulling the screens down in front of their shops, some locking up anything the Macoute could take away. There was a television set on at one corner, propped up on a small card table, with a group around it watching for an announcement. As she hurried by, the station was showing the green and red flag at sunset and playing "Yellow Bird" over and over again.

For an hour she lay with her sisters in the back room, feeling the warm wet heat of Betti, the youngest one's, head rested against her bare thighs. It was amazing to her that Betti could not feel the life that was stirring inside her stomach and had now stretched down past her loins and into her legs, making them warm and even hot at times with the trembling. In the moony air of the room she imagined that anyone who came that close must have felt the change that was there under her bones, that the night outside and the thick shaggy pines and the silhouettes of the hills were opening up, breaking from their skin like newly sprouted flowers. Even the air, it seemed, would announce her secret.

But her sisters slept on, and by the time the moon had disappeared above the single window her brother Marc came in and kicked at Betti to get her to give up her place. Betti complained as she always did and Marc would soon make noise, Fia knew, because she could smell the alcohol on him already, and because there was nothing for him to do at night now since losing his own job except drink with his friends. So Fia volunteered to leave first and even as she said it she did not believe it would work so easily; but the sisters rolled a little and Marc only sat down heavily in the space she had abandoned without speaking.

Outside the moon was suddenly visible again overhead and hugely bright, nearly full with long bars of cloud surrounding it like a quilt. The ground around the clumps of houses itself was a soft gray, as if the light had sunk into the dust between grasses and stones, into the almost-white strip of road that led off into the hills. Marc's friends were still sitting around the foldout table playing dominoes; one of them watched her tying back her hair rapidly with night-eyes that were sunken and curious. In silence she passed by.

Halfway in a warm breeze came up and Fia knew Papa Legba was comforting her. It was perhaps he who had made the curfew, made possible the dim early secrecy of this night. The long dry grass lay down on its sides before her, ripples and paths opening up and inviting her legs into the fields and out into the cover of trees. She was being invited out into converse with the *loas,* into trysts with unseen whims and powers. But she stuck to the path she already knew, though at times it was not a visible path but just bare, pebbly ground, and when she found the *houngan's* house the light was on.

The *houngan* was inside his kitchen, fixing something to eat. Normally his maids fed him but tonight he had told them he was going to bed and then had lain unsleeping for almost an hour. His house was made of concrete and had electric fans in the windows; some said that he was Macoute and that was how the money came to him, but the *houngan* himself said that he gave offerings every morning and every evening to Baron Samedi and Kouzinn Zaka, saying, if you are pleased with this *houngan,* give him rewards. And the money came to him, whether he asked for it or no. This second theory was held by as many people in town as the first, and his great estate was taken to be a sign of the success this *houngan* enjoyed with the spirits. Fia waited outside his porch until the *houngan* came outside to eat his sandwich and watch the stars.

"What you want?" the *houngan* said. He had been startled at first, holding the sandwich up in one hand as if it would defend him. Three or more strings of amulets wound around his neck, their heavy ends rattling and tucked inside his shirt. "What you want here?"

"Miguel Jeanfils put something in me," Fia said.

□   □   □

Even the next day when the shops were forced open again by military order and she walked out to work she could tell the quick surprised life was no longer inside. Instead there was a silence in her now, a hollow at the middle: and when no one was looking she felt around the skin of her stomach and her inner legs with careful fingers, listening for any sound. But there was none. Her legs were her own again and the private knowing place of her loins was quiet, that place that had been opening out, she felt, eagerly like a flower opens, and warmer in her hands at night when she lay down with the second life that had been concealed within it. She was undone.

For a week and then two weeks she did not think of Miguel Jeanfils, of his happy smile that was not quite a smile, of the windy, bent feeling he brought to her, like the bending of the dry grass, silver and lean under the moon. She did her work and at lunch break she sat, sometimes, at the edge of the water overlooking Ile de la Tortue with Ane Baptiste, watching the clouds that had not broken into rain, and did not think of him. Her father had gotten in a fight down at the granary where some of his friends still had jobs, and her brother, when she saw him, smelled badly almost every day now. His face was beginning to sag underneath itself like a weight and she passed him wandering through town sometimes, doing nothing, his young features falling slowly and full of the quick red anger that could rise up in him at any time. The friends had stopped coming around their place at night. Fia bought food for her father and sisters, or gave her father the money directly when he showed her his tired hands; always, it seemed, whatever she had went straight out of her grasp and into theirs. And still she did not think of him, of Miguel Jeanfils and his long neat shirts and the ties he sometimes wore, of his intelligent way of speaking with French and English phrases about *Capitalism* and *Indigénisme* and his knowledge of politics and his future.

The *houngan* had given her things to drink that would make the child go away: some of them were sweet and tasted like spiced liquor, while others were thick and terrible to taste and had hard pieces in them she had to chew down. He had held both her hands and made her sit inside a *veve* ring while he pulled her around in a circle from outside it; and he had given her a small picture covered in cloth which she was to keep in her pocket but never to unwrap and look at. She had offered to pay him from her work but the *houngan* had taken no money, saying he had known Erzulie Dantò wanted him to help a woman who would come to him carrying something in a sack, it was why he was not allowed to sleep, and he assumed it was she whom the *loa* had meant.

It was on the night of the third week after she had been cured of Miguel Jeanfils' touch that she had the dream. At first she did not know she was dreaming. She was sitting, awake again in the hot midnight air, in the back room with her sisters. From somewhere in the fields behind their house came a sound, a quiet, wavering note like someone weeping. She rose and went out back (this was where she decided she must be dreaming, for the house had no second entrance) and followed the dim, far-off wail through the hills and under the clicking lances of palms all across the island, it seemed, until she found it: her own child lying in the grass, its bare arms and legs soft and unprotected, its delicate skin faint against the moonlit earth. It was crying like a bird.

After that dream Fia began to think of the touch that had been inside her as *her child,* the child she had given away. It seemed to her to have become something more than an abstraction, more than just a piece of Miguel Jeanfils. It grew to a living thought in her mind, *enfant,* a piece of herself and not just of something passing through her. Her baby was to have been a vital breath that came from her, a statement and a purpose from the center of her being; had she had the child, she felt, that act would have made her the live heart of something of which she had always been on the periphery. It was not her father's *bébé,* nor her brother's *bébé,* nor her sisters' *bébé;* none of them were clever enough to have done what she had almost done, none of them had the intelligence nor the will. Suddenly her family seemed to her slow, dull-witted, unable to take the flame as it passed by their lives once and perhaps not again. She thought of them as dirt, heavy and unusable; and her *bébé,* as a shaped thing that came from the dirt but that she herself would make clean and new and sudden in the midst of them all. She wanted it back.

In the afternoons under the hot sun she listened with her hands to the silent place near her stomach, listened and prayed to Legba for a sound, a pulse, some unperceived thing: but all was silent. She was a quiet, unoccupied well, she was an absence where once there had been breath. And her wind-child, her cloud-child, she had given it away. She wanted to be full again of rain and the sound of rain on the muddy streets; of the sound of the people calling out from the market stalls at noon and past noon; of the hiss and clack of banana trees and stream-rich hills. After work she went down to the water where horseshoe crabs were grappling in wet bunches. She parted their carapace bodies with her bare toes and watched the upturned legs struggle and search the air for the lost touch. She opened the little picture wrapped in cloth that the *houngan* had given to her and that she had tied to the inside of her skirt, and looked at it: a blue-and-white painting of Erzulie Dantò, Virgin Mary, made in one hundred little chips, torn from some magazine and stuck onto cardboard. She threw the image into the waves, listened to gulls shrieking down at her from the air.

□   □   □

When Fia found the *houngan* the second time his maids were standing out front like sentinels, one holding a broom wrong-side up. Fia asked where the *houngan* was but the women said nothing, staring wordlessly at her even as she walked between them and into the house. The *houngan* was in a garden behind the building, tossing coffee grounds over a large black cross. He turned toward her and in his other hand she saw he had bread, pieces of which he was tearing off and soaking in the cup. The *houngan* looked at her from out of his red, sagged eyes for a time; then he continued what he was doing. Fia went inside.

The walls of his house were a crazy collection of trinkets, paintings, photographs, sheets of *Le Nouvelliste* and *Bon Nouvèl* and *Newsweek* tacked up with inscriptions written on them in French or Creole, or sometimes both. There were arrows and names drawn by the *houngan* at the bottoms of some pages, and several of the smiling photographs had been marked *OK* or *maji* with a kind of ink-brush. There were oil canvases of the sea, and of fishermen, and of the crucified Peralte. There were feathers of flamingoes, and conch shells, and jars full of sand, and bead-strings, and rosaries with crosses on them and off them; one entire wall held shelves of tiny lit candles burning in colored glass. The *houngan* came inside.

"What you want?" he said.

"Want my baby back," Fia answered, staring at him straight on. "Wind-baby, moon-baby..."

"Want what?" the *houngan* barked, incredulous. "After I did women's work for you and took that bad touch away..."

"Moon-baby," Fia said, standing firm in the place where the *veve* ring had been. "Trees-baby, dream-baby..."

"After you come to me saying, take it away, take this bad touch away..."

"Grass-baby... rain-baby..."

"No way now," the *houngan* said lifting his hands in an angry blocking gesture, then going into his kitchen and looking for something to eat. "Ain't no way now to undo what's done." He shook his little head.

"I brought *kob*," Fia said. She laid everything she had earned that month on his glass-topped table, everything; the green bills smiled up at her hand uncritically. The money faces understood what she was doing.

"It won't take money," the *houngan* said. "Ain't no way now."

"I brought *kob*," she said again, reaching into the other pocket of her skirt and taking out the rest of what she had saved, all she had saved for her sisters and her father's hands and for them all, and laying the money down on the glass-topped table. The *houngan* came and looked at the pile of money. Then he looked at her thin body as if he had not quite seen it before, chewing slowly.

"Only one way," he said.

□   □   □

When Miguel Jeanfils returned she almost laughed at him. *Imagine,* he said to her in a sweet piping voice, *this little flower laughing at me!* And he had tried to make her laugh as well, called her the little flower while he started to light a *Comme Il Faut* and then put it back, but she never laughed. He was like a light that had gone out from her now, a dull candle that has been licked and will no longer sputter. Fia sat at the shore rocks and watched his lanky, childlike legs carry him away over the breezy grass. How could she have loved him? Her friends had been right. He was nothing.

And she: she was renewed, a well-bucket drawn up full, and more than full. In the days now after work she sat on the rocks and looked out over the water toward la Tortue, Turtle Island in the north, and watched the evening light changing to storm-light and knew that it was inside her, this light. She knew that the Ile and the giant tortoises who swam over there and screamed when they dropped their yellow-gray eggs bloody in the sand and the sand itself were inside her; that the people who lived all around her and the rich ones and the poor ones were inside her as well. The Macoute had come back through to close down their shops again, and this time Fia stood right in the road looking at them, and all at once they were taken up inside her. She had them in her body, in her knowing place, and they could be no more outside her or away from her than the air she breathed. The whole street laughed as they saw Fia possess them all. Nothing would be a fear any more. Nothing would be anything now, because she had all things in herself. She sighed, resettling her thickened woman's haunches on the hard edges of rock; watched the mounting, pained clouds over la Tortue draw close. She was giving birth to the world.

Ava

She woke early, before the guinea fowls even began their long, weird salvos from inside the pen, and stood in the center of her single room alone and naked in the far southern light. In America she had never slept naked; had felt, as her parents had instructed her, that the sacred temple of God that was a woman's body was to remain covered even at times when no one other than the owner could see it. This latter notion she had added herself, interpolating a further restriction that seemed to her to flow naturally from the general rule. It was a habit, like cleanliness or cultured speech, that a spiritually-well woman nurtured, the pride of humility. But in St. Marc all that was different.

For a while she had tried to maintain her old, American ways—she had worked hard and early to clean her hospital whites to a starch freshness before the day's duties began, to remove any bloodstains, or body fluids, or stains from the soil-marked hands of her patients, or from her own soil-marked hands when she spent whole days laboring in the gardens or replanting sections of stump trees that the villagers had broken into at night and torn down for charcoal. She would keep two sets of clothing for herself each day, one in which to sleep and one in which to work. The sleep clothing she cleaned as regularly as the work clothing, though she had no lovers and had had none, and though no one other than herself would see the clothes in which she slept.

That had been for the first year, almost the whole year, and by the end of it the work was so great and took such devotion that she began to let her evening ritual slip. Once or twice a week she would fall to her sleep lying down on the hard, springless mattress without washing her bed clothes in the steel tub out behind the mission rooms: first because the washing had to be done by hand, and now more often than not her hands were baked red on the top-sides by the sun, and the hard, abrasive bone-soap hurt them in the pores, and the bottom sides were very often aching from hours of planting or pulling and cleaning old roots or transporting stretchers or making food, and the flat, wide muscles at the base of her shoulders felt like a runner's legs after running. So she let the evening duties lapse, once, and then again, falling into unconsciousness only in a large and nearly shapeless shirt that was grandiose enough to cover her privates when it hung down, and telling herself that decency was at least accommodated by this, as virtue was, in the end, a state of the heart. Always at least she wore the long shirt.

Then one morning she woke naked, with the high weird challenging of the guinea fowls outside, and found she had cast the shirt entirely off herself in the night. She was lying uncovered in bed with the tropical sun making its first watery slot-lines across her belly. It seemed to her she had been lying that way for some time, the sun touching across her bare legs and her womb-space, and a vivid thrill was appearing in the bones of her legs and somewhere inside her center, a thrilling stir of something. She stayed in that position for some time, listening to the others begin to wake in their rooms, some of which were only separated from hers by very thin walls, erected out of quicklime in the first months when

they came here and there had been several more volunteers than
the building could accommodate.

Those initial people had all dropped out now, returned to different service or left the devotion altogether. She still received
postcards from a young man with whom she had worked through
one long, faintingly-hot summer and who had an excellent eye for
impromptu diagnosis: he had been a secular and devoted to what
he called the "international cause." They discussed the calling
often; he ribbed her kindly, and she knew she was charmed by his
nonspecific complexion and by the black hair that emerged from
the collar of his tee-shirts, his black head of hair that was like a
mane it was so free and sweeping and not at all coming away with
age. But while he was political she was more devoted to the
beauty of God and God's will, and told him so if he became disre-
spectful with his jokes. He was stronger and rose earlier and took
on more responsibilities than the rest of the missionaries. But
when the summer was over he was gone with the others, back to
the U.S., where he now lived in Philadelphia and worked part-
time in an AIDS clinic, and wrote to Ava about his devotion to
the people and his longing for the day when they would rise to
their rightful place in societies all over the earth, shaking off their
chains and burdens like summer straw. That was the phrase he had
used. Mail came through St. Marc infrequently and it was difficult
to tell when the postcard had been written: its glossy flip-side of a
beach in Delaware with the white women bathing in banana-yel-
low suits seemed bizarrely out of keeping with her life, and she
had not answered it. That was the last she had heard from the boy
with the quick, bright eyes set in deep features who had held such
promise for the mission, but had broken quickly, *jan fey yo ap
tombe-a, the way palm skin breaks away*. She thought of his eyes
then and how it would be if he were in the room with her, how
the eyes would be on her, and the living thing in her rose to a

flush of blood and a tingle like shame across her sunburnt arms and the back of her neck.

For a while then she had forced herself again into the routine of sleeping with at least the wide shapeless shirt covering her body; but the heat was so extreme and the air was unbearably solid and massive at night, when the stars over the Atlantic seemed like pinpoints of ice at unreachable distance. Gradually she began to sleep naked more and more often, keeping the shirt near her in case something, she did not know what, would occur in the night so that she might be called down into duty or someone (the door really had no lock, other than a formality that anyone with a strong shoulder-push could snap out of place) would need her. She would stand by the sill of her window in the nighttime quite unclothed and watch the stars over the *Golfe* and feel from time to time the slow heat-wind that moved through the palms and around her like a presence—like something that soaked into the skin and into the person and made you not cooler, the way American winds always had, but denser, more rooted into the earth. Quietly she waited for the new growth, for the sap, the change.

The Spiritual Exercises

The first time Fr. Maretin saw the girl, he guessed her to be fifteen. He was incorrect by one year, though the records, often written in a semi-literate Creole, were only approximate. Her skin was a faintly lightened brown, the color of milked coffee, and she cared for it, he thought, as a real woman would. That was not the way with so many of them, who let their skin become like their hair, or like their worker's hands, which were not good hands. The only pure thing he had seen on the island was their dress, which they kept flawlessly white by grinding the cloth down with stones. It was a practice in which they would take no instruction, and one that mimicked, ultimately, a kind of fanatic asceticism. The first time they saw him in his vestments, a foolish man in the confessional row made an approving motion with his hand for the others to see—imitating the rock used to make an impressive white.

She came in to the hygiene class and right away he could tell she was not in need of improvement. He could smell the cleanness on her, like fresh bark or the beaches after rain. The others needed to be told again this week how to boil the water before cooking in it; yes to bathing but no to bathing in stagnant pools; no to eating the *fresco,* flavored ice that often had microbes, sold by the man who sat next to the fishery. No to the alcohol, *Barbancourt* and *Prestige,* that was such a burden down here, keeping good men drunk and preventing the women from being productive. Yes to Christ.

She listened intently to everything he said that day and at the end of the class she stayed in her chair after the others had gone. He thought that she was going to speak; perhaps it was only the Creole that was a barrier to her, and something welled inside him at the thought. Had she seen him noticing? From far down inside him his heart beat darkly, but she rose a moment later and left without turning her head.

□   □   □

Then she was gone. For days he did not see her again, not even at the food lines or in the late afternoon when all the work-ers gathered outside the fences and they shut up the compound to prevent beggars coming in after hours. One summer before they had built the fence the Macoute came by joyriding late at night and paid a visit to the *blans Américains* by throwing lighted wads of cloth and stones through three windows in the rectory. Fr. Maretin didn't believe they actually wanted to hurt them: when given a despotic power, even physically mature men behaved like children on the loose. Nothing was badly damaged.

At the end of the week he was serving Communion in the chapel. It was nearing twilight outside, a red low sun streaking the walls around him through the slatted wooden shutters. They received the sacred bread from a church distributor in Duvalierville every third week along with oil, powdered and non-perishable foods and UNICEF crates, although of course it had not been blessed yet when the sweating men slumped the pack-ages down on the mission steps. Fr. Maretin lifted out a piece of creamy consecrated host and she was there.

She looked as if she had prepared herself for the occasion. Her clothes were tan colored and neatly wrapped around her body, so that he did not get the sense that they were fastened anywhere, but intricately teased about the torso and the belly like a sheet wrapping a sleeper's form. Her hair, too, was concealed, that hard brushlike hair that he did not like in the others, behind a wide, fat cloth that was pinned somewhere in the back. Her cool forehead shone.

"Close your eyes, child," Fr. Maretin said in French. "Say *amen, Father.*" But she continued looking at him. "Close your eyes," he said again. "Close them and think on your sins." But she continued to look at him. Her eyes were very clear and dark, and she stood with her mouth open and waited for him to do it.

"Voici le corps du Christ," he said, placing the bread in her.

□　□　□

That evening after he closed up the compound gate and returned to his rooms she was there, standing outside the doorway in the shadow of a mapou.

"You need to leave the mission, child," Fr. Maretin said. Inside him the new thing tumbled, startled and afraid. How long had she been hidden there, like a strange growing? "All the workers need to leave after sunset. You can't sleep here."

"I want to get religion," she said.

He looked at her waiting there in the feathered softness under the mapou, leaned up with her back against the stretching bark in the off-white dress that seemed to glow a little under the branches, and her arms spread back and holding onto the tree as if in constant and unbreakable union. He could not see her face, but he sensed that on her face was the same patient waiting she had shown in the chapel.

"In the first place, you are to address me as *Father* or *Père.*

I am the senior official on this compound..."

"I want to get religion," she said from the leaf-shivering cover. "I want to come over."

"Come over?" Fr. Maretin said. "Come over from where?"

"My mamma was a *mambo*. My *grand-mère*, she a *mambo* too. They want me to become *mambo*. But now I've seen you and I want religion. I went up into the hills to think, and now I want religion."

"You want me to help you overcome the curse of vodou?" Fr. Maretin said, straightening. "To escape the curse that is on this land and on your people? You want to embrace Christ as your true lord and master?"

But her face was black in blackness, ink on velvet, just watching him and giving back nothing.

□   □   □

After that he started seeing her around the mission once again. Through casually-dropped questions he discovered that she assisted with the nurses in the care units, bathing the patients who could not bathe themselves, taking away their refuse and disposing of it in a sanitary place out back. She carried stretchers, and once he saw her operating a string of blood tubing. So she had some education.

That night when he returned to his rooms she was waiting again outside.

"I want religion from you," she said. "You got to give it to me."

"Come inside," Fr. Maretin said, only she didn't move, staying coiled there under the mapou and the shadows trembling across her body. He could feel her eyes working.

"I am going inside," he said after a minute, his face averted. "I am an old man. I have served on this island for eleven years and I need sleep when time permits. In the morning we are going to be digging trenches for the replanting of small shrubbery outside of town. The more shrubbery you have, the better off the water supply will be. The better off the air will be. You people need to learn discipline. And waiting." But the hidden face was silent. He went inside.

When he had finished his evening prayers and had washed his body and his mouth Fr. Maretin undressed for bed and began a meditation. His meditation that night was on the sixth rule of the *Spiritual Exercises of St. Ignatius,* but his meditative practice was impure, and his mind would not stay on the different interpretations of the line *that descended on him in the shape of a dove.* He opened his eyes and she was in the doorway.

"You said you'd give me religion," she said.

"I said no such thing," he hissed. "Food, yes. Shelter, where and how it is appropriate. I have entered into no pact with you."

"You came to me up in the hills," she said. "It was you I saw. You told me to come to you, and you would make me new. The *houngan...*"

"What the *houngan* does or does not give you to drink, or what mistaken visions you had afterward, is none of my business," Fr. Maretin cut her off. But she laughed, shrill and alive.

"*Houngan* never give me no drink," she smiled. Even her teeth were straight, he thought; straight and clean-looking, like American teeth. "I got the second sight from my mamma, the *mambo.* She got it from her mamma, the *mambo.* Now it's in me. And I went in the hills and asked for a sign. Gimme sign, Legba, I said, gimme sign, Erzulie Freda. Didn't eat or drink nothing for a week. And *you* came to me."

"Turn away, child," Fr. Maretin said. He intended to dress again but the girl would not turn away: she remained standing with her gaze fixed on him. *I will not play these women's games,* he thought with sudden irritation, rising painfully to find his things in the half-light with only his nightshirt on and his rosary hanging underneath. His knees and his wrists ached from carrying seed bags that day along a path where the truck that usually brought them had broken down, and the dim room swayed before his eyes. But he did not want to turn on the overhead light now because it would have forced the generator to kick on in the back-house, and that would wake the others.

"Take this and read it," he said to her, handing her his copy of the *Exercises*. "Can you read?" But she only looked at him with her strong gaze. "Then you can't read," he said. "Is that so?" But she: and the eyes. "That is so," he concluded. "Well then. Sit, here, with me. We will read together."

Then she sat, not in the proffered chair but on the floor, curling her torso perfectly around strong legs, legs that Fr. Maretin knew carried her as infallibly through the hills where insurgents and counterinsurgents walked as the sacred spaces here of the mission, curling her dress beneath her. He told her of the vices of man, beginning with the gravest: carnality; and after that: despair. He told her that she had a haven in Christ before she was born into this godless place, this nighttime world, where the people had been corrupted across the years by political desire and the false hope and ways of Satan.

"Don't tell me no *politik,*" the girl said, like a clap of hands. Her face had not broken for an instant from him, her wrapped body at peace on the hard matless floor in a way his bones would never be again. "Don't want to hear no *politik* from you. You got to give me religion."

"They are one and the same," Fr. Maretin said sternly. "You people will never be free until you accept Christ as your guiding principle in life, neither the slaves of this world nor the incarnations of the Evil One. Papa Doc was a vodou practitioner. A *bokor.*"

"Don't tell me no Papa Doc," she said. "You got…"

"Papa Doc was a slave of vodou," Fr. Maretin cut her off forcefully, and leaned over and gripped her leg in strong fingers. When he touched her body he could feel the dark thing leap inside him, the new hated life that was terribly in him, racing closer. He took his hand away. But she had felt it.

"You not such an old man. Father," she smiled.

□   □   □

At the end of the month they were holding Mass when a young man with a red bandanna tight around his throat stood up from his folded chair and started shouting. *American pigs,* he cried, drawing a long thin finger in the air and singling out every missionary at the altar one by one. *Ale Fe Wout-du Vye Chin Amerikin Ke-wye! Aba! Aba!*

He started repeating the curse over and over, throwing in disconnected pieces of other phrases like *sacred class struggle* and *pwoblem klas sosyal,* his implacable finger making its slow sweep across the altar. Fr. Maretin tried to continue reading from the liturgy, but the shouting was like thunder in that little slatted building: he could see the nurses and orderlies were afraid to do anything. Wearing blue jeans and the bandanna, the man was probably tied to the Macoute, or wanted to be seen that way. To try and silence him could incite further actions. Fr. Maretin himself had been shouted at before, but only sporadically: a Duvalierist slogan exploding from someone's lips as if they themselves could not help it, as if they had to rush from the chapel to escape its influence in their mouths. But this one was not stopping.

"When he had given thanks and praise he took the bread and gave it to his disciples, saying, take this..."

"*Se pou Envayise yo mouri!*" the man cried louder, starting to knock the feet of his chair against the wooden floor boards. "*Koupe tèt!*"

Others began joining in. The man who had started it was gesticulating with his arms now, shouting to be heard above what was turning into a general confusion of voices. "*Allez! merde de putain, Américains, allez blanisme,*" he stormed, repeating phrases he had been taught somewhere, but his was just one of the voices now. Some of the others were trying to silence him, but there was a growing unity of people muttering the dangerous *Aba Envayise, invaders get out,* as if all had secretly been thinking this but had not willed it into expression until now. Fr. Maretin looked up into the crowd and raised his hands in slow appeal but before he could find words he saw her: she was there, seated in the back of the chapel, her hair wild and untied now, something in her watching face that lived and danced.

Two missionaries tried to remove the shouting man, but as soon as they came close people rose up to defend him, and then what Fr. Maretin had prayed and sworn he would never let happen became real: the shouting man struck out with his fist, hitting a Dutch medic named Rieule, and when Rieule stood up again he was bleeding a bright line from one nostril down across the white of his shirt. There was an eruption.

Fr. Maretin moved to defend the monstrance with its wafer of holy bread that had not yet been removed, grabbing the ornate circle that was to be processed down the center aisle of the chapel and holding it to his chest. Someone was pushing at him from two different directions, trying to take the monstrance away; his feet gave out and he felt himself being forced to the floor. He had the liturgical book in one hand and his fingers were slipping on its hard smooth cover; he could not hold on to both it and the monstrance. There was the sound of exploding glass: behind him the supply boxes were broken into and people started grabbing at the unblessed bread, stuffing loaves and hunks of it into their shirts and under their arms. A large-breasted older woman wedged a rind of bread down into her dress front, the effect almost comical. Fr. Maretin looked up and the man who was trying to pry the monstrance away grinned widely into his face. The man was laughing and saying something over and over but by that time the chaos was too loud and the words fell painlessly across his ears.

□   □   □

Well after midnight a car came into the compound, stopping at the gate to break it open, then motoring around loudly inside the mission grounds and gunning the engine underneath windows where medicals and priests were sleeping. At one point a bottle of something popped like a bomb on a stone wall: *Barbancourt,* Fr. Maretin thought, or *Prestige.* He listened to the sound of the motor, recognizable from its hollow thundering as something old and imported from America, as it skidded around the compound, without rising from his cot. Overhead the ceiling fan turned unresponsively in blank shadow.

The sound stopped once under his window; Fr. Maretin heard them talking loudly among themselves in quick, indecipherable Creole.

"Hey, Father White," one of them called into the air, the distorted English slow so he could understand it. "Hey, Father White! What you doing with our good black women? What you doing, old man?"

There was laughter and, he thought, something other in it, something mean and stronger than mean, something with a raw cutting tooth like the tooth of the half-buried saw he used to come across on his own father's farm in southern Kansas, jutting up blood-colored and frayed at the edges like the teeth of a dangerous thing that was sleeping in the earth. For several hours afterward he lay and remembered the land where he had been a boy, the man with the sad, restless face who had raised him alone, in a place where the earth was stiff and dry and needed to be broken with sweat every season to make it bleed up the life. Long after the motor had driven off again and there was only the shadow of the mapou standing outside his window he could still hear that young voice calling: *Hey, Father White. Hey, Father White.* It sounded to him like the calling of a bird.

At a Ceremony in the Hills

The shirtless boy delivered a competent smile, the state of his teeth notwithstanding, and disappeared into the crowd. LeFay had six shots left before he would need to return to the little yellow car with the *jounalis* sign that could be popped up in one window and the fractured rearview and rock-dents from a time when being *jounalis* was not enough. Things in Port-au-Prince were getting so tense, with the power shift having started but not finished, that he had been stopped three times on the roads tonight, once by a group of drunken men who were building a makeshift roadblock with gasoline-soaked tires. When they saw he was *blan* they let him through, slapping his back and joking, LeFay giving out unfiltered Camels to the wine-stinking faces and acting as if they would all be friends the next time they met, knowing full well that if he were to drive back along the same road in an hour and a half the same men might feel it best to shoot him through the head.

So there was that, the issue of exactly how he was going to make it back to his hotel, or whether it would be logical to even try and do so before daylight. The roadblocks he had seen built by such makeshift committees had the same rough status as parties, and generally burned down to a foul-smelling crust before morning, when the worn and now painfully hung-over vigilantes would make their way home or lie down by the hissing remains of their handiwork to sleep it off. He could spend the night in an open graveyard, something he had done once already. Or he could continue to travel up north all the way to Arcahaie, but the car he had gotten at the airport did not handle potholes well, and if there were roadblocks being built in one direction by people who were neither Macoute nor Aristide nor *Kominis,* there would be roadblocks farther on. He checked his upper pocket for remaining Camels and ducked under the hanging arm of a tree.

The festival was well under way, and from the looks of it LeFay imagined that the dancing had started as much as an hour earlier. From this side of the scrub brush the firelight was conspicuous; it was what had first drawn his attention, on a night and at a time when the flicker and shake of open flames meant tipped cars, or military actions, or necklacing. He had sent back photographs of men who had gotten on the wrong side of such parties once; they had appeared again in the ripped-open manila envelope on the bed in his hotel room with a letter from the management saying the mail service to America was experiencing some "discomforts." Next he had tried sending them through the Belgian Embassy, and when the same thing happened he included them in a return-parcel of empty medical containers shipped in and out by WHO. He received a wire from Jason Stuart at the *Post* the next week saying *Can't Use Too Bloody Send Coconuts,* meaning that America wanted something touching the heart but not quite so offensive to the eye. America wanted only to be indignant about Haitian misrule, not revolted.

"Because if you were truly revolted," LeFay said aloud, "truly and deeply revolted, you might feel, being the household gods of the West, that you had to do something about it. Am I right?" At the time he had sat on the same hotel bed and read the simple sentence over two and three times, and then he almost felt like laughing and then he definitely did not.

Now he made his way closer in, feet sweeping the unseen grass. A cracking sound came from overhead and LeFay ducked down, the mass of celebrants who were visible around the three fires doing the same, but it was only a few Japanese-made bottle rockets. When he looked up again someone was laughing at him; the children had migrated up into limbs of the mapou.

"Take my pi-shur, take my pi-shur," a young voice chanted. Three of them dropped down and LeFay recognized one he had seen already in town, without any obvious parents around him. A scattering line of silver going back across his tightly-curled hair gave him away. The result, perhaps, of a long fever.

"Say *do you love me,*" LeFay said in English, crouching down on one knee with his camera out. "Say *do you love me* for the American papers so they can all see how innocent you are." He poked at the silver-streak boy, who giggled and then impulsively bit at the side of his own hand. LeFay saw the spider-thin drool coming from inside the mashed fingers as the excited boy chewed, his wet eyes locked on the *blan* in a kind of rapture. *Typhus,* he now thought. Something that had taken the speaking part of the brain with it.

"Take my pi-shur," the leader shrieked again and the others moved in beside him, the mute child biting his fingers harder and hopping a little in place like a small bird. LeFay put the safety on and pretended to snap pictures of them all: faces and eyes leering out from the winking dark.

"One, two, three," he said. "Click click."

"Gimme *kob!*" the first one shouted. "Gimme *kob!*"

"No *kob,*" LeFay said. He was looking around now, back at the dancers and the flickers of ash that traveled up through the trees and into the star-busy sky. Then the children were gone.

Closer to the dance-floor—a palm-swept area of trampled dirt and whitish *veve* powders laid out in lines, on top of which the dancers were rolling their bare feet in the slow, preparatory movements of the trance—a group of drummers beat out cultural hypnosis across stretched skins, to some of which long stiffened strings of cattle hair still clung. LeFay listened: there was merengue in the air as well, coming from a transistor radio somewhere, giving a beat to a different group of people farther off in the grass, their forms only a quick flicker of motion in the shade. Over the drum-dancers a tent had been erected on poles with the *poto-mitan* in the middle for spirits to descend. Its billowing roof caught the firelight and heat and turned it into the rapidly unfurling shape of storm clouds. LeFay crouched down.

"Fête pou Azaka?" he said to a small group in general, offering out a hand with three slim cigarettes in it. He would have to be careful: the pack had felt nearly empty when he fingered it.

The man sitting closest to him looked over for a moment and then smiled and took the cigarette and began sucking on one end unlit, as if unaware of the procedure. The others either refused, or refused to see him, because their heads did not turn away from the dance. One man kept a simple variant of the loud drum rhythm on his bare thighs with quietly slapping palms.

"Pourquoi la fête?" LeFay asked the one who had responded, careful to show no offense. *Why the party?* He had guessed Azaka just because that was the harvest spirit, keeper of fertility and births, and something about the gathering here seemed like an earth festival. It had that communal feel.

The man holding the cigarette in his mouth smiled back and rolled the paper cylinder up and down with his tongue; LeFay was uncertain as to whether he was being mocked.

"You're not a big conversationalist, are you?" he said in English. "Born stupid?"

"Donnay mwa Difé," the man said, pointing to the tip. LeFay found a match and lit the Camel, and the man smoked and returned to watching the dance. After a minute LeFay moved on.

In the center of the sweating drum-dancers a heavy woman was making space for herself with her arms, swinging them not in violent but decided gestures. Several others recognized the character of her actions and backed away to give her room. She was not young and not pretty, LeFay thought, and her face had a stern kind of mobility, like a declaration. Her eyes were shut tight as she stamped a deepening rhythm that traveled up through her cloth-wrapped thighs, the rider *loa* mounting her like a horse.

"Who's coming out?" LeFay said to a man seated on an overturned orange crate. A bottle of wine was going around and as LeFay watched, a young woman who was so feverish her shirt was soaked down to her visible nipples took a drink and handed it on to the next person, not even wiping the mouth of the bottle.

"Ogou," the man smiled. He was old and in the half-light the skin around his cheeks and chin had the appearance of a worn gravel path. LeFay regretted for a moment not having a camera strong enough to take that image and save it. There was a roughened beauty to the contours of the aged face that only an artist or a philosopher would ever appreciate.

Coconuts, he told himself. *Mysterious dance under the waning moon; all the standard racisms. America wants to think of these people as children.* The old man did not look at him but did not seem to mind his presence. He squatted in the grass, in clear view of the dancers and the tent, resting on his heels and waiting for the possession.

After a few minutes something else mistakenly entered the body of the dancing woman, who now had the *veve*-ground all to herself, and when the *houngan* who was seated at the back of the stage sent it back out with a sharp slap to her forehead the crowd all laughed. A small wind gust came and bent the ascending trails of live cinders down like an arm. When LeFay looked back, the scene on the dance-ground had changed: the woman was now on her knees, her own palms open and slapping something down into the dirt.

"Koupe. Koupe," she chanted, and LeFay moved a little now to see better what was in her hand: a broad knife. With the sharp end she was striking divots in the powdered earth.

"Koupe," the old man next to LeFay said, his voice so sudden and loud LeFay felt something inside him jump. The man, wrapped loosely in a thin blanket rather than a shirt, had not looked away from the stage.

The *houngan* left the stage and LeFay realized the merengue was gone now; there was a strange near-complete silence among the tall grass and underneath the limbs of the trees, and the emptiness between stars, the only sound coming from the again straightly-rising lines of cinders that grew from rust-eaten trash cans in which burned charcoal and sticks.

"Qui est..." he began, but the old man did not turn his head, did not move his eye, and LeFay could not speak, the sound of that quiet anticipating crowd hushed him and quite suddenly he was glad he was crouching in the dark, glad he had not made himself visible to many. He had a strong feeling about the *houngan* and the woman stabbing the knife down, a feeling stronger than he had felt when the drunken men stopped him and clapped killer's hands against his shoulder blades and called him *ame* and *cheri* from mouths that stank like death pits. He crouched in the shadow.

The *houngan* returned with a white goat bound at the hooves. On its belly crude spirit-marks had been painted with some kind of oil.

"Set kou'd kouto, set kou'd ponya," came a shout from the

crowd, followed by another. *"Koupe le tèt blan."*

He'd heard the phrase before, seen it spray-painted on walls in the most embattled regions of the capital and surroundings: *Koupe le tèt. Cut off their white heads.*

"Koupe le tèt," the old man said, half-loud, not looking away.

The *houngan* held the living animal partially aloft by its front hooves and the possessed woman, spirit of Ogou on earth, spirit, LeFay knew, of vengeance and the setting of rights, cut off the animal's testicles with a sawing motion and showed them to the crowd. The goat gave one kick and then began to bleed, its eyes two sightless spots stranded now among the greater unseeing.

LeFay got to his car and the group of men standing in the shadows he had expected, had known, would be standing in the shadows there by the absurd yellow rental with the *jounalis* sign badging it and the U.S. sticker in a silver oval on the back were not standing there. He walked around front with his heart talking and talking up inside his head and the hood had not been popped and critical wires spread uselessly like eels: he got inside and put the key in the ignition and when it started he looked for a moment at his fingers shaking against the wheel.

"Christ," he said. "Christ. Christ."

He dropped the emergency brake and turned to glance behind. A small figure was standing there, one arm bent at an odd angle and the hand jammed up inside the working mouth.

"Take my pi-shur," the voice said from out of the nothing, backed by firelight. "Do you love me? Do you love me?"

The Woman and the Man from CARE

The woman and the man from CARE were standing in the prow of the boat, overbalancing it but not badly, so that the empty motor-hole took in water at first, but little more than a greenish plash. After they had settled the young priest entered, more dexterous with his tan, muscled legs spread wide in the manner of people used to stepping into small craft. With them all aboard the keel descended below its usual mark, which concerned the young priest somewhat to see: this was his boat, insofar as it belonged to anyone, and the responsibility for keeping it afloat was his as well. He had petitioned the American Embassy and then the consul to the archbishop several times before getting it, a torn and unusable hulk when it finally arrived. He himself had repaired it with his knowledge of boat-finishing from the summers he had spent working his way through college around the New Jersey shore. And it had served them well: there had already been a time when a helicopter relief drop came through and three-fifths of the packages went into *la Golfe,* floating like little buoys and soaking up salt.

Now he was concerned about putting this much weight in her but it had been communicated to him quite clearly that they were to impress the representatives from CARE when they arrived and to show them every possible evidence of work well done. Once he had restored it, the bishopric was more than happy to claim his boat as evidence of the zeal and devotion of their foreign missions.

They cast off lines and let the mood of the water begin to take them outward, the little fishing skiffs and the hand-mades bobbing farther out with their stitched-together sails looking like flags on the brightness of the water. Then they were in a good bit deeper but the boat felt fine, and the young priest was able to relax. The man from CARE was extremely fat and had a strong bodily odor that drifted backward from his squatting form.

"You can see the curve of the land starting from here," the young priest began, gesturing across the line of sand that ran into red scrabbling rockpiles and out farther toward a slash-pines hammock. "There's actually an amazing effect that can be seen from the water at day. It's akin to a mirage on asphalt, only the evaporation line just above the water acts as the reflecting surface. It can look like the island continues on indefinitely."

"I don't see fauna," the woman from CARE said to her coworker. "Fauna doesn't check."

"We're in what's called a dead patch at the moment," the young priest said, his arm locked naturally around the tiller now that the wind was starting to appear. He felt good in boats, had all his life, since the days when he worked ten- and even fifteen-hour stretches for the old man who put him up in the room where his deceased son had once lived, a room kept exactly the same as it had been the night the boy died, as if in homage, so that the young priest felt at nights as if he were sleeping in the presence of something sacred. Sometimes he mused on the notion that the sea at Manahawkin was what had actually brought him into the priesthood: those wonderful tales of Jesus as a fisher of souls. It was an idea that pleased his sense of the aesthetic. "As strange as that sounds. There's been so much polluting of Haitian waters by American business concerns setting up shop here..."

"And European," the fat man appended, one solid hand raised in the attitude of an instructor.

"Yes, and European..."

"I've even heard the Japanese built something down here," the fat man said. "Process the stuff almost in American waters, only to sail it all the way back to Japan, for Christ's sake, then reroute it east again along Amero-Sino trade routes. Unbelievable."

The young priest winced a little at the profanity, let himself seem occupied with the sail.

"The whole place is the albatross of Napoleon, anyway," the woman from CARE said. "I really think *they* ought to..."

"In the summer there are dead spots in the water," the other woman piped in, making it sound as though she meant to pick up the young priest's interrupted comment. She was a social worker who was raised in Minnesota, so that before they understood her intensity the others joked with her that choosing work in the Caribbean hardly constituted sacrifice. She had bright, surprisingly fluid features that showed the intelligence that animated them, a thin, strong face and a small mouth, with a look of vague accusation that rested there when not in use. "No fish or plant life at all. It seems clear that's the result of outside pollutants."

"It's ironic," the young priest agreed quickly. "This looks like the clearest water here. Yet it..."

"Have you run pH tests?" the woman from CARE said. She had auburn hair that frizzed up terribly in the humid air, and battled to keep it down with a kind of strengthened hair net. That morning when she had woken up for the first time in La Saline the fat man was virtually on top of her, trying to enter her while she slept. She didn't mind; he was older and unkind and she was also unkind, and there was an understanding of that fact between them. When the room service asked her if she needed anything she had turned the angle of the bathroom door so the young black employee in his spiffy suit could see her naked. The fat man had loved that.

"We have," the priest said. "It's on the high side, higher than would be regulation, if there were any regulations. Also the pH goes up naturally in the summer so any corporation would be able to say…"

"The question is, do these phenomena impact negatively on fishing-based food productions?" the woman from CARE asked, rearranging herself a little in the hull. The fat man was looking out across the water, seemingly immersed in his own thinking; his upper lip pursed out into a little shelf.

"They do, yes."

"And how exactly? What are the vectors…"

"These people are *starving*," the mission woman said, abruptly. The young priest had hoped she wouldn't do it. He was aware of her temper, knew, he believed, of the passion of her commitment to the poverty and persecution and disease and incredible disparity between the dirt-floor *have nots* and the fifteen- bedroom *haves* they had found down here, so much of which was a result or even a direct intention of American policy. When they had come across a cocaine mill last year in the hills not ten miles from mission grounds, with workers openly processing the plants and bagging them in burlap sacks labeled with U.S. customs numbers, she had taken a photograph of the smiling men standing around their work and mailed it to the embassy, asking if they at least got minimum wage. He had wanted her to stay behind while he took the CARE representatives for a quick jaunt up around the lip of beaches where last week they had found a dog floating in a sewage pipe, hoping the visuals alone would make their point. But he did not need a confrontation.

"If you look up here..."

"Excuse me?" the woman from CARE said, ignoring the priest. "Did you say these people are starving? Is that what you just said?"

"Yes. That's what I said."

"And you think we don't know that, I assume. From your tone of voice, I assume you think we're unaware of the socio-economic position of this country."

The mission woman tensed her jaw and waited. The young priest could see she was in no way intimidated by the hostile words, but was only holding herself back by her awareness of him at her side. They had had discussions regarding relief workers before.

"That wasn't what I meant," she said slowly.

"That most certainly was what she meant," the woman from CARE scoffed, vaguely in the fat man's direction. That morning in the hotel room he had made her call back the *marabout* bellhop and ask him a question, any question, in English, so long as she referred to him as "boy" at the end of it. She did it and the fat man laughed until his belly shook against the frame of the bed. The woman smoked a cigarette in the nude looking at him and when she was done she flicked the spent end onto his chest.

"You can see," the young priest began again, but the fat man, whose thoughts he most wanted to impress, was not looking at him but out still across the water. "You can see the number of crab and lobster pots out here. Every five to ten we see of these for the rich represent one for feeding the local mouths..."

"Did you hear what she said to me?" the woman from CARE said. "Did you hear her say that? 'These people are starving.' Like she's trying to teach us something here."

"It wasn't what I meant," the mission woman said.

"It was what you meant, sweetie. Oh, it was."

The young priest rubbed the sweat around his eyes: the reflected sunlight was burning into them badly and he had left his sunglasses at the compound. And the minute he looked away from his coworker he knew it was a mistake; but it was already too late. He felt her almost jump in her seat.

"You're damned right it's what I meant, you bourgeois bitch," the mission woman said. "You're goddamned right. I meant to say you're a lying cheating bottom-of-the-food-chain thief who doesn't give a damn about these people or anything except how much you can get away with. I meant to say you're bilking the system for every goddamned penny..."

"Stop!" the young priest cried. "Stop this!"

"Jordan!" the woman from CARE cried. "Did you hear what she called me?"

"Yes," the fat man said abstractedly.

"She just called me a bitch! This goddamned holier-than-thou..."

"You are a bitch, Emilia," the fat man said calmly. "Be quiet, now, won't you?"

The woman from CARE flushed visibly underneath the burned skin of her face and looked at the fat man with the expression of someone biting into something. When she spoke again the words were very slow.

"You, priest," she said. "Turn this thing around. We're going in now."

"No we aren't," the fat man said.

"The hell we aren't! Who the goddamn hell do you think... do you think I won't tell them what you are? Do you think these goddamned crusaders wouldn't like to know what kind of man you are? And what you do with all that precious charity money?"

"We aren't going in yet, Emilia," the fat man said.

"And why is that?"

"Because a man is presently being murdered there."

The young priest's eyes turned to where the other had been looking, across the water and back onto the ochre-white strip of beach. A group had gathered there and had a thin shirtless man on his knees in the sand with a tire forced down around his torso. They were beating him with what appeared to be strips of rubber.

"Oh, Jesus," the young priest said. "Oh Lord. Oh my Lord."

The man on the beach fell on his side and the others began kicking at him, raising little flurries of sand. When he fell over it became apparent that he was completely naked.

"You were watching," the mission woman said, the rage in her voice suddenly gone empty. She looked like someone had just drained the essential being from her in one fluid rush. "You were watching this happen."

"You would hardly suggest getting in their way, I suppose?" the fat man said, turning to the others for the first time. His eyes were water-blue and sparkled perceptively under the shadow-line of his hat. "With guests in tow?"

The young priest was trying to maneuver the boat around but he lost the wind and for a moment they sat idly in the water. The man on the beach lay now on his side, no longer moving.

"Stop," the young priest cried, reaching out his hands from a flurry of bent and useless sail-lines as if to cast them across the impossible space to the small crowd that was already dispersing. "Stop this! Please stop this!"

The tire was set aflame and the remainder drew back, disappearing into the streets and toward the treeline while the man on the beach flashed and burned. The wind came again and started taking the unguided little skiff westward away from the shore, bending the sails in the same direction as the thin smoke that was beginning to rise.

"You'll smell it in a minute," the fat man said to his coworker, resettling himself into the prow. "I saw this done once in Soweto."

"I don't want to smell it," the woman from CARE said, looking elsewhere. "This whole island already stinks."

Lòt Bò Dlo

Gras-a-Dye sat once more on the stony part of the docks, looking across the harbor to where it opened outward into the deeper, waiting colors of the Atlantic. Close by, hugged up against piers that were little more than sections of rotten wood, torn orange crates, canvas bags, hung the squat box-shaped boats tarred black against the sun. The one from which another skipper had been quietly removing his possessions all morning was a day-fisher, roughly thirty feet long, and inside it, Gras-a-Dye knew, twice that number of people would pay to stand on a certain night at a certain time. The skipper would take their money, disappear from this place, and they would take their chances.

He was without work this month. He had been a pig farmer before the job with the church; he had four pigs and a sow and four of them died of swine fever in one year and when the last one died he had been so hungry he had cooked and eaten the poisoned flesh out over a charcoal pit he dug deep into the ground, praying to Agwe and Sen Jak Maje not to let him contract the *chalè*. He never got it. On the morning three days later when he knew for certain he did not have the fever he went and threw coffee grounds over a carving of Baron Samedi at the roadside, and then he went to find the rest of the pig he had buried in the charcoal pit on the chance that it was still edible. Hauling it up out of the pit with a rope, he found the sour-smelling flesh blossoming open with colonies of ants.

Now he was without work except what the church allowed him to do, sweeping up and sometimes helping to paint and strap together sections of ready-wall flown in from somewhere to assist in the new buildings they were making. He had a sister in Arcahaie and some cousins there, and he had already been, on foot, to stay with her and see if there was work; but there was none, and the sister had three small children by a man who, when he came home, would not shake Gras-a-Dye's hand. He left that place and worked for a while with one of the cousins in a paper factory and then on a sugar milling plant, but that had ended when the white Britisher who owned the mill got word that an underground smuggling operation was taking his sugar into the D.R. There had been no operation, but the white Britisher had fired every Haitian on his crew, saying *there are a dozen where you came from* to every man as he went out the door. Now he was back at the water, the *gourdes* in his pocket most all of what he had left, and a strong back still and arms with nowhere to use them.

In front of him where he sat on the shell-littered rocks the men, men with sweat showing in great looping rounds underneath their armpits and up the spines of their shirts and the muscles in their forearms standing up like thick roots, worked on their floating boxes and slapped each other on the flat areas of their backs while the women went and cooled off for a while in the flickering shade. Gras-a-Dye had been watching the secret exodus now for some time, returned here often to sit when he was not working himself. By sundown at least one of the boats would be out in the water, taking the first thousand yards or so slow, judging how far they had gone by the color and pitch of the sand visible underneath them, lest the hull collapse right away and all the men need to swim around and draw her back in. If the hull did not split and take in water and the balance was good, and the central mast sat stable in its barrel-shaped holder with the stitch-sails hanging from it like crazy flags, they could be out of sight of the land before the moon appeared over the ocean. After that it was in the hands of the sea.

□   □   □

When Gras-a-Dye was a child his father had spread ocean-salt across his brow and sat him in a *veve* ring to see which way he would turn, and pronounced to his mother that the boy had *water in the veins;* the ocean being a strong pull on him, and his most powerful *ezil* being *labalenn,* the whale. It was the source of his name: Gras-a-Dye, for *Thanks to God,* because his father had seen the power of God in his son and refused from then on to call him by the original family name. Instead he would of necessity be praying every time he spoke his own name, the praise of God would be always on his lips. He had been singled out.

As a young man Gras-a-Dye felt his father's indicators had spoken true. He fished for years, when they still owned the skiff that had been worked by his father and grandfather before him and in which the two of them would ride, his father's alert, powerful hands only skimming the top of the water at the downstroke of his paddle, and waiting without moving or speaking in the skiff until the water was a single sheet transparent as air. Only then would his father begin calling the sharks.

He, Gras-a-Dye's father, was one of a line of such men; his grandfather had been a *griot* as well, and the blood had been passed to Gras-a-Dye. His father—riding with Gras-a-Dye in the skiff that had been built to hold only two people, could not hold a third, because the one was to be always the father and the two was to be always the son—sat cross-legged in the prow and waited without speaking for minute after minute before anything discernible happened. The older man's hands, formerly so alive and skilled to the task of paddling, were transformed in the hot water-reflected sun into loose, gentle things; not in the effeminate way, though, but like sudden new places of tremulous, untouched skin. His father would hold the palms of his hands out over the water so the surfaces just met, his digits leaving ripple-lines circling gradually outward. And he would sing.

The songs were stories, stories of family past and world past, stories from the days before Macoute and Zinglins and the occupation, and the occupation before that. Stories of Henry Christophe, the slave king who hung French men from poles in the street like flags; of the Chanpwel who walked up to the front doors of the plantation houses and dropped human hearts onto the painted steps and left them there for the owners to see in the morning; and how the plantation owners fled or were themselves the source of the next heart. Of Faustin Soulouque and times before that time, when earth had not been *Ayiti* but *Ginen,* another place vast and *lòt bò dlo,* across the waters and somehow underneath them as well. How the invaders, both black and white, had taken the people from whom Gras-a-Dye and Gras-a-Dye's father and Gras-a-Dye's father's father were descended into slaving ships and fed their withered bodies to the gods who followed in the traders' wakes.

In time he would blow the horn. The horn was made from that of a bull with carvings wound round the outside and the inside: images of Agwe dancing with Erzulie: of the lovemaking of Samedi, who was Death, with the Horsemen, who were earth in her manifestation now and earth in her manifestation before, the earth of the others and the people out of water-time. His father blew the horn with the *ason* rattle tied to it and Gras-a-Dye blew

the conch, its crusty fleshlike rim meeting the edges of his teeth
and the salt taste of it leaking up, working the end with his mouth
and his own hands gripped over the fat swirl of it and making the
sound, the two horns, son and father's together, calling the god.

It always came. His father was an excellent speaker for the
people, excellent speaker to the gods, and in time the calling
would be answered by a single lean blue motion, the dorsal fin
not even passing above water yet: the shark, its yellow-mottled
underside showing as it glided and the solid, horselike eye, passing
alongside and underneath the skiff without the smallest flexion of
its one continuous muscle. When it came, Gras-a-Dye the child
sat still in the stern of his father's boat and in his gut came a sinking, a warming and a sinking sensation, a pit opening up inside
him and the light and the level power of the day sinking in, drawing him down into himself in fear and into a space beyond himself. His father's head did not bend to watch the god pass, did not
wait to see it circle around, if it circled; instead he breathed into
the horn again, its long, sonorous and somehow personal voice
against the still water, and in time the god would return, long,
blue-skinned, its locked obsidian eye watching from just above the
colorless sand.

Always at these times Gras-a-Dye felt nearest to the old man.
At other times, on land and in the daily work that both of them
did, Gras-a-Dye scraping and cutting the fish and packing them to
be taken to the morning market, they were just two men: working, near each other by the proximity of their needs, two men
who labored out of the sea. Later when Gras-a-Dye began to
travel he would remember how it had been, sweating next to his
father in the market stalls alongside a dozen others, shouting out
the names of their catches and a fair price always somewhat higher
than what they expected to receive. But calling the god they
seemed to fuse, as the voice of the horn and the voice of the

conch fused in the still, translucent air that blended into and across the noon gulf.

He was a young man still when the sharks stopped coming. "It's the disease of the land," his father said to him, when he, Gras-a-Dye, was adult enough to know words like *Duvalierisme* and *Dimanche;* when he was broad and strong-armed from having grown up working any job he could get on the docks and had seen larger men, stronger and more adult men, cut open by the Macoute much the same way he would open up a flying fish, and signs propped next to their bodies burned or hanged or crouching still in the street breeding flies: *This is From Uncle Sack.*

"The land is broken down," his father said, by this time an old man and no longer a magician but an eccentric and a holdover from a generation of superstitious men who, Gras-a-Dye now believed, had allowed for the political state of things in his home country by lack of critical intelligence. Gras-a-Dye knew the old man at last and at times was disgusted by him. "The land is poisoned by its own bile, and Agwe will not touch it," the old man said, his mouth working poorly a handful of *biswit.* "The people are not touched by the gods."

In those years Gras-a-Dye had been to vodou ceremonies in the hills where his father sat in the corner of the *peristile* drinking cupful after cupful of clairin, drinking until Gras-a-Dye was amazed that he did not simply sag onto the earth like a wilted growth. People in the broad red-dust of the dance floor would be dancing slow and dream-like until one was caught, fish on a line, by something unseen in the air and would begin gyrating more pronouncedly, almost with a power, and he would hear his father say *"Gede, go, Gede, go away now,"* and push away the dancing, hip-thrusting woman or man who would have come near him. And the *loa* would leave, the spirit would release the body, and the dancer either fell to the floor and was carried off or returned, mute and dazed, to the slow, torpid dancing, the rhythmless all-at-once motion, until his father had a hold of the presence he wanted to see, the correct spiritual manifestation for which they had lit the fires and candles and arranged and executed the ceremony. "No more," the old man said once when the young Gras-a-Dye had asked him when they were going to another dance in the hills. He had not asked it again.

When Gras-a-Dye was seventeen his best friend told him a secret. "I'm becoming *kominis,*" the boy said, suggesting to Gras-a-Dye's mind that this was a condition that moved over one slowly, that there might still be room for recourse even halfway in. But the boy smiled wide and had something bright in his eyes, a bright strong secret power, like the eyes of the dancers when Dantò or Azaka moved inside them.

The friend started inviting him to meetings of the Communists, people who wanted, he explained, "to turn Haiti into Cuba." They explained superstition to him, and the repressive power of religion over people. Haiti needed to be liberated. It could be done, the friend insisted; in fact it could not in the long run be avoided, because the dialectic of history determined that the *politisyen* would not always be suppressed.

Gras-a-Dye had never heard such terms used and knew that his friend did not know them either; knew almost from the beginning that other people in the group were teaching him the *konstitisyon kominis* and how to speak its language. In class while they sat at the square, uncomfortable wooden desks and listened to the teacher reciting phrases in English—"My name is Pauline," she said slowly, with a thick accent, "My name is *Pow*-line,"—the friend was there, in another part of the room, looking over at him in between lessons and sometimes even during lessons with the smile and the awake look that said: *Kominis. Yes. Kominis.*

Then one day three men in blue jeans came into the room

and started asking students' names. The students were afraid, and abruptly Gras-a-Dye saw on his friend's face not fear but something beyond fear, something so vastly beyond and shining that it was almost impossible for him to look. When the friend's name was mentioned the others pointed to him and the men went and took him by both his arms and hauled him out of his chair and toward the door, grabbing as well a second person whom Gras-a-Dye did not know. Gras-a-Dye waited for them to call his name, waited in his stuttering heart, but it never came. When the white teacher tried to stand in the men's way and shouted something at them, one of the men hit her next to the eye and she backed up rapidly saying "Oh! Oh!" and holding her face. The friend did not come back.

But now Gras-a-Dye understood the old man. The old man was a mystic, superstitious, part of the capturedness of the past that had haunted Haiti and kept it from becoming modernized since the almost-liberation in 1804. It was the beliefs of such people that allowed the island to be played as the dupe of nation after modernized nation. It was such beliefs that had weakened the people and allowed for the police state to evolve.

He continued to go to the meetings of the *kominis* friends, though he could not have said exactly why: in a fervent exhilaration he thought perhaps the *kominis* disease was in him now. At first the others had eyed him warily, asking a great many questions about the Macoute who had come to the school and what they had said. But Gras-a-Dye felt nothing; he answered their questions without hesitation, and with an odd feeling, now that the exhilaration was gone, that none of these things could touch him. The fear he had felt sitting in the classroom seemed very far away, a strange fear like part of another person's experience. He continued to learn.

As they met and talked in back rooms after selling hours, or in small rooms that seemed to belong to no one in particular, it began to grow inside him, a sense of what *lòt bò dlo* was and what it could mean; a sense of *libete politik* and *pwopriete pwive;* he wanted to contradict the *kominis* and have *pwopriete pwive;* he wanted to *own* and *make.* In America he felt, obscurely, that he could do these things. There would be more knowing, more education, the vast mills and granaries were there with food for everyone, the swelling mammoth buildings, the *libete.* He yearned sometimes for *lòt bò dlo* with almost a physical sensation.

Then he would contradict himself, just as quickly: there would be no freedom until there was general access to the means of production. There would only be interim states, places larger but essentially as despised as Duvalierville; the reign of the proletariat was nowhere. And he thought it was better to be here, working only for himself when work came, living "close to the situation," as his *kominis* friends had said, though he did not feel necessarily close to anything. And still at times he yearned, obscurely.

Toward the end of his life the old man would not look any more at the sea. He had not been out in the skiff in many years. Gras-a-Dye was aware that his was the first generation to have broken the continuum, he was the first *ounsi* descendant of the grandfathers to refuse his post, to refuse the old superstition, and the two-man skiff hung unused and corrupting on a strut by the side of his father's house. The old man ate only fish now, and had to have it brought to him by a neighbor's little boy. His flesh was decrepit and unstable on his bones, and he spoke in a low mutter like the murmur around the base of a beach-fire. His hands, which once seemed so soft and knowing gliding across the water, were frail, strange things. In his presence Gras-a-Dye felt more and more often a mounting disgust. After a while when Gras-a-Dye came to see him the old man would not even lift his head; he stared fixedly in front of himself, facing away from the water and speaking his low, unheard murmuring, his hair salt-white and even the ends of his fingers uncertain in the dust.

Gras-a-Dye went to Milot. He worked in the salt mine there for a year and then another and was there when the single, unsigned message came to him from the Belgian man who owned the mine and who had never addressed him nor anyone he knew by name: *your father dying,* and he took the money he had earned up until that week and went back to the edge of the water and the little falling-down quicklime shack where the old man was. He never knew how the message had gotten to him, or who had sent it. His father could not write, and there was no one in the little town who knew where Gras-a-Dye had gone, nor who knew his father, after his mother had died. The old man was sitting in the center of his shack, squat-legged on the ground, the neighbor's boy watching them both from the end of the room. Gras-a-Dye came and sat next to him.

For a time their eyes did not meet and the murmuring mouth of the old man did not break its rhythms; *he's telling the stories,* Gras-a-Dye realized, *still after all this time he's telling the stories,* and the old man reached over and took his hand in a cool, stiffened paper one that was as coarse as a palm frond and said: "Put mine in with the others. Put mine in with the others," and Gras-a-Dye promised that he would.

He had never done so. After the old man died Gras-a-Dye buried him next to his mother's grave and paid the undertaker for a small somber headstone with the family name. He did not return in a year's time to dig up the magic man's body and take the whitened skull back to the sea and stack it with the others, grandfather and great uncle and great grandfather, and the one even before that which was small and brown and crumbling in on itself, where they all stared out of the mapou tree at the sea with the salt air crusting up in their eyes. He did not believe in such observances; he did not believe Haiti would be served, nor the general proletariat, and even if his father had been right and the land was poisoned, choked on its own corruption, that would not be righted by a maintenance of magic and the long misunderstood nighttime of the past. It was over.

□ □ □

By evening the jury-rigging of the craft was almost completed. Seated by the water still, Gras-a-Dye watched the men and women dispersing back into the streets and the long colored paths that led to town, one or two of them building small fires on the beaches to cook some dinner. He did not feel hunger, some part of him realized, for the first time since he could recall. When the moon rose oblong and glaring above the placid distance of water he watched it sail, scudding across a mild ocean of cloud, until it was low and gone on the far horizon; the beaches now empty save for a few sleeping forms and the occasional upward lancing of a spark from the slumbering fires. In the morning color washed gradually and then with amazing abruptness across the eastern horizon as if promising hope, as if the sun itself would act the portal: then it too rose and the true heat of day was returned.

With the first heat came the same men and women, this time with full sacks and suitcases brimming with clothes, photographs, two men carrying a chair between them. The women began coming out from under the shade of the palms wearing bright skirts and hats as if they were walking to a wedding; the men shirtless now in the morning heat and one of them, a bearded, narrow man with visible stringlike scars running up and down his chest, slapping the young women on their bottoms as they clambered into the boat. Now that they were actually breaking the law they moved with a new insistence, a close knot of people suspended between two dangers and trying to gauge which side was worse. He watched them move themselves into less space than, as a fisherman, he knew would hold half so many with one quarter the weight. And still the boat stayed up, and the ropes were brought down, and swimming men worked it out into the deeper water by pushing its sides along the sand, stepping high in the water to avoid the coral, the box-shape turning a little from side to side in the waves and then making for deeper water.

Gras-a-Dye rose, walking down to the pebbly part of the shore where the men who had been guiding were walking back toward dry land, rising back up into the sun with water cascading in falls down around their belt lines and cascading again down their legs. He removed his shirt. The men slapped him on the shoulders as he went past and said some things and then he was in the water, standing in the pebbly-sandy water and his pants going dark and close around his skin as he went in deeper. He walked in the stumbling dream-walk of swimmers until the icy water was up against his belly and the pants were too heavy on him, and then he pulled those off too, and naked he began to swim, his length spread out now, moving easily with strokes that brought little splashes and his muscles starting to jump and come alive as he worked them more strongly. The men standing on shore, seeing him, began to shout something, and despite the danger one made a long, protracted catcall through his hands while the other laughed, but Gras-a-Dye was close on the little ship now, swimming up alongside it with the people so close to each other they could all only stand calling down to him from the side. The man who had brought a chair was without his chair now and looked unhappy. Gras-a-Dye swam alongside the little box and looked up at them and listened to them shouting for him to come up, reaching hands down to him, but he did not answer. He swam with the boat until the water became deep and choppy and the man with scars across his chest, who had produced a cigarette from somewhere, looked over the side at Gras-a-Dye and removed his cigarette and spat in the water and disappeared again among the bodies.

Gasping now Gras-a-Dye tried keeping pace with the boat, his strong legs going *kick-kick* in the water as the stern moved farther away. Far enough out that he was past the waves, the salt taste up in his nose and lips, he watched the box grow smaller and smaller in the rocking blue expanse that had no visible end. He watched still swimming after it until it was a mute wedge on the greater blue of a horizon that was not split from the air but merged with it, his tired legs now kicking and resting and kicking under him as he treaded far from the land.

Gras-a-Dye, he thought, as loud as he could think it, sending the words down through his legs and out his wide-kicking feet. *Gras-a-Dye, Gras-a-Dye.* His body tiring, tiring but refusing to return, he prayed the name his father had given him, the name that had been his own but was never his name, the name that was both a prayer and a tale and a disgrace and now was the only thing that remained. Gras-a-Dye prayed it, prayed it with treading arms and back and the strong working of his heart. And after a time the long, sand-blue form of the shark came and hovered, glancingly, its rhythmless motion beginning between and around his legs.

Lasyrenn

In the southwestern sloping end of the island of Hispaniola there are two places called Fond-des-Negres and Fond-des-Blancs; no one, including the socio-historists and the socio-linguists who have written on Creole and its tapering roots in Old French, have fully explained the names. They seem to mean "belonging to the whites" and the same to the blacks, from the time when one could distinguish them by race; "completely white" and "completely black"; or, and this almost metaphysically, "source of the light" and "source of the dark." The crude translation among foreigners was "white ass" and "black ass," and these were the terms in regular use.

The people who lived in Fond-des-Blancs were used to seeing workers come through from time to time. Their trucks were invariably old and rusted and gave the impression, even to people for whom a car was a luxury and a walk of three or four miles carrying grain sacks not uncommon, of coming from an America not terribly interested in her own goodwill efforts, regardless of how they were touted in the *Bon Nouvèl*. They were used to the vague smiles and the Jesus talk, and the handouts from relief groups, which tended to be beef jerky sticks and bottles of Gatorade. These the men up in the afternoon hills ate and drank with slow lank jaws while they watched the *blans* sweating and handing out pamphlets. Later they took turns throwing rocks at the Gatorade bottles lined up on the tops of fences.

These trucks had that same welded-together appearance, driving in the heat with the dust yellowing up their painted sides. As they got closer it was possible to see, held down with burlap skins and roped onto the body of the vehicles themselves, the shaggy heads of several baby palms swinging crazily from their backs. The addition of the shaking, clattering greenery to each truck gave them a ridiculous air, like vehicles dressed up for a *ra-ra* somewhere.

They drove through the village center, the women standing by houses with their babies slung in cloth sacks not returning the waves given by one driver or even moving, save in the slow rotation of their heads, to catch the image of the trucks kicking up their dust and bouncing the green spikes along. When they had passed by the women returned to nursing their babies or stirring *fritay* with sticks. The two trucks stopped on the outskirts of town.

A young white woman with the muscular, well-tanned arms of a field worker descended from one truck and two men from another, one of the men sucking on the end of a long strand of hay as if he were imitating the American bumpkin. Although he was still quite young he held a Ph.D. in environmental science and had been involved in the drive to oppose straightening several rivers on the Florida gulf coast, a move that had been originally proposed to increase hydroelectric power. The environmental impact of the project, especially in the depletion of certain breeds of fish, had become a bugbear for the power companies; and the young man with the Ph.D. had made something of a name for himself and the organization for which he worked. That, and his minimal knowledge of French, was how he had become attached to the Haiti program.

"Site C one one one seven A," the man said, as if this settled something on which he had been musing. The woman kissed him.

"Just where you left it."

She had her degree from Brown University in Rhode Island, and had afterwards moved to the outermost tip of Massachusetts to become involved in dolphin tracking; now she wore a small pin of a dolphin on the lapel of her shirt, which some of the local women had mistaken for a *gad,* the charm of a power-animal. It was a misunderstanding that had pleased the young man very much.

They hiked to an area a little way back in the hills where the trucks could not follow, searching for and finding a series of holes they had dug the week before. There were seven in all, lacking two that had refilled entirely when a large sluice of red earth coursed through the site from a higher elevation. The young man had said before that he had not meant to give it a whole week between digging and planting, but the delay had been unavoidable; beggars had broken into their base camp the first night and stolen a month's worth of provisions.

"If the oldwood on the incline had been left standing, the slide itself wouldn't have happened," he observed. It was a vicious cycle the locals had gotten themselves into. Cutting major sections of a limited growth supply removed all root support from unstable dry-earth systems. No roots meant frequent slides and even less stability for the remaining trees. The deforestation had been even more starkly visible from the air when they came in than from the ground: great strips of land rolled off toward the cerulean water like a slowly crumbling sand pile.

"More pollution, more soil corrosion, more desiccation," the young man said, happily. "No trees, no rain. It's really a great example of *laissez-faire* economics at work."

"*Lasyrenn,*" the woman said.

"What?"

"It's what those women at the market were saying when they saw my pin. *Lasyrenn, lasyrenn.* I wonder what it means?"

The baby palms were loaded into rolling flats they had built themselves out of the pieces of old bookmobiles, left over at the schoolyard in Cotes-de-Fer from a failed literacy project sponsored by the Catholic Church. The woman called to the workers in the second truck, who assisted in lift-rolling the trees out of their roped-in places and getting them into the carts, and rolling them across the bumpy rising-falling ground toward Site C one one one seven A. Halfway into the hills they had to stop to rest, although the track from where the trucks were was only a few hundred yards long. One of the workers took out a cigarette and lit it.

"I wish you wouldn't do that," the young man said. "We're here to clean and green."

The worker smoked his cigarette and looked unblinkingly forward. Eventually the young man looked away.

"Let it go," the woman said.

They continued with the haul and when the trees were in place and standing upright in their spots, they gave the appearance of a little ordered grove in the midst of a greater brokenness. Everyone was sweating heavily now, and the young man squatted down in the soil.

"Okay," he said. "That's almost got it."

"That's almost got it," the worker who had been smoking said. He was leaning up against the side of one of the trees with no expression. The skin around his jaw was wet and marked with beard stubble.

"I said that's almost it," the young man repeated, slowly. "All we need to do is assay the soil samples…"

The worker took out another cigarette and lit it.

"Do you have to do that?" the young man said, angrily now. "Do you really have to do that?"

"We're finished here," the woman said. "Let's all head back to camp."

"We're not finished here," the young man said.

"Finished," the worker called to the other men behind him. "The lady says we're done." There was a small cheer from the other men.

"We're not done," the young man said more loudly, trying to speak to all of them at the same time. "We need soil samples…"

But the worker who was looking at him with lank, expressionless eyes only waited until he had finished talking. Then he pitched his cigarette away and walked back to the second truck.

"Let it go, John," the woman said. She squeezed his arm.

"Let it go? What the hell…"

"Please."

"Why are you so…"

"Just please."

As they drove back through Fond-des-Blancs the *fritay* grills were now visible flickering in the dusky light that came across the evening hills. They were in time to check the first site, site C one one one seven B, which had been planted by a different team the month before. When the young man pulled his truck off the road the other truck drove by without stopping. The driver shouted something at him as he went past.

"The bastard," the young man sneered. "He's not even going to stop."

He idled the truck and got out to stand in the middle of the road. He sincerely hoped he was visible in the rearview mirror.

"You look kind of foolish like that," the woman said.

"Kind of foolish? What do we pay these people for? He's not even going to..."

"Let it go, John," she said, calming him with one hand on his sleeve. "Let's just check the site and get back to camp."

"Why are you so eager to protect that... *goddamn son of a motherfucking... whore?*" the man shouted, suddenly. He was hotly red about the neck and cheeks now. His shirt felt like it was buttoned wrong.

"Because I overheard them discussing what they found yesterday. They were talking about it over breakfast and they didn't think I was listening. I didn't want to tell you."

"What they found?" the young man said, still speaking too loudly. His own voice sounded stupid in his ears. "What did they find?"

"Someone hung a body from one of our trees. Some say it might have been against us, others think it was just infighting. They went out and cut it down this morning while you were asleep."

The young man could find nothing to say. "Good God," he managed, eventually.

"Apparently it wasn't the hanging that bothered them so much as the... when a naked man is left like that, he gets an..."

"I have to go apologize."

"No you don't. Not really."

"I didn't understand. They're good men and I didn't understand."

When they made it back to the base camp night had already fallen and several of the others were seated around a beach-fire built on driftwood. They sat quietly eating their dinners, staring into the flames. The young man asked for the whereabouts of the workers who had been on the drive with them. A Haitian man named Alourde gestured at the water and said something in rapid Creole.

"He's in the water? I don't understand."

The young man walked down to the edge of the ocean, where a more complete darkness than he had ever seen covered the sand and the audible curling waves. It was so black he realized after a minute of straining that he was looking at pinpoints of false light fluttering inside his own eyes. There was a singing sound coming from the invisible surf, a song that turned occasionally to bellow. Only when he wasn't looking directly did he now and again discern the white form of the man splashing naked in between the waves.

"Leave him alone," the woman whispered, appearing at his side. The young man's heart leapt panicky at the suddenness of her voice, as if she had materialized out of nothing but filmy space.

"He's drunk. That's against the rules. Listen to him. He's drunk out of his mind."

"*Lasyrenn,*" she mused.

"You what?"

"*Lasyrenn.* I asked Alourde about it. He said it's a mermaid. A kind of sea spirit. He seemed to think it was a great compliment."

The young man was silent.

"Come back and be with me when you can," she said.

The woman turned and walked back up the beach, disappearing utterly and eventually reemerging in the fireglow. The young man watched her lean form reflecting by the fire, seeming very much at her ease. He wondered how much he knew about anything that happened in the world around him, how much less of the unseen world inside him. In the greater absence behind his back he could hear the troubled waves; it seemed that the ocean itself was singing.

The Beauty of that Face

She loved him immediately. Nor was it just the love, Ava thought, that Christ had shown was to be found in all human beings, that dimly-seen reflection of the one ancient and unchanging face. From the moment the small group of women carried him in hanging motionless between them there was a kind of flash inside her, something she could only compare to the dry lightning they saw sometimes out over la Gonave: lightning that was always a lie and a deceit because the rain never fell on the parts of the island where it was needed, and when it fell the soil couldn't hold it and ruptured out like a broken sack, and the land died and the people, in time, died with it. In five years of living down here and doing the work of a missionary here, that much had been made clear to her.

He had been beaten about the face, and after those five years she had also started to be able to tell what had been used just by examining the marks that it left. This time it looked like someone had taken a wooden stick to the skull, knocking in the tender skin where it is thinnest over the cheekbones, and knocking the cheekbones a little as well. There were some other cuts and swelling around his shoulders but that was probably just from the scuffle.

His teeth were all in place, and so it appeared that whoever had done this thing, what they had wanted to hurt mostly was the eyes. Which they had done.

"A little present from Uncle Sack," Jons said. The boy couldn't see anything with the swelling blocking his eyes out completely, so they laid him out on a stretcher and carried it into the room used for examinations. Ava tried to speak to him a few times, and Jons tried with his better Creole, but there was no answer. Still she could tell just by looking at him that he was there, was conscious: she didn't think there had been brain damage or severe concussion. His breathing was deep and regular and the sweat was standing out well all over his chest the way it does after a beating, when the body is trying to reject all the toxins that it itself has started generating in a crazed attempt to wash over the hurt places.

"Where does he come from?" she asked.

"They found him out in a sugar cane field this morning. His family did. He had a brown grapefruit sack tied around his head, with a cord, too tight for him to get it off. When they cut the sack off they found this." Jons gestured toward the body as if it were something on display.

"A Macoute sack?"

"Is there any other kind?"

But there were other kinds, Ava knew, though they had argued the point. After the Tontons made it a popular method of dealing with their opponents, other groups had started using the sack. Anyone could get an old bag from any vendor in any market: the material itself didn't matter. It was the gesture that mattered. And the effect it had on people, she felt, and the fact that in the end, it wasn't ever anybody in particular who had committed these crimes. While some debated whether Uncle Sack was still tied to Duvalier or running itself, Ava had seen a more fatalistic read in the eyes of the people she knew in town. To them, Uncle Sack simply *happened.*

"They must have held him down and just taken shots at his eyes," Jons said, touching at the massive swelling like a baker testing risen dough. Ava flinched in her new and sudden emotion, but the boy didn't move under the Swede's broad fingers. Only he kept up his strong, audible breathing and the heavy sweating that was marking all his bloody shirt now like he had been splashed with something. "It's too puffed up to do anything right away. We'll have to get some ice, wait until the swelling clears enough to keep us from doing more harm than good. And hope the eyes aren't dead underneath."

He was speaking in English so the boy couldn't understand but still she felt it was bad for him to have been speaking that way, so much without feeling, even when hopeless situations appeared at their doorstep all the time. When she was still a new volunteer a man had come in with his leg broken open, a compound fracture he got trying to hike along one of the drop-off hills where crops could still be grown without ownership of the land. He fell and the leg got caught under the exposed root of a tree stump, something that had been cut down almost flat to the earth, and his body twisted the other way and the fibula popped out at the knee. He had stayed like that almost for a week because he didn't want to get any help from the *blans Chrétien,* and when he couldn't stand the pain any longer he went to a *bokor* who packed the exposed bone in animal dung and tied it tight with rags. By the time he came into the mission the gangrene was all the way up into his hip and Ava had known just by smelling him that the whole leg would have to come off.

When she passed through the foyer a woman in a yellow bandanna and earrings started grabbing at her coat tail. She was unable to follow the words: something about how she must *look in his hands,* or *look at his hand.* Ava pulled herself away and the old woman started keening, right there in the front room. The whoop was picked up by some of the others who had come with her, and then by some women lying in cots. When she managed to get into the back room again they were almost in unison.

"It's all right," Jons said. "That's not the death whoop."

"You can hear the difference? It sounds so... absolute."

"They'll get over it," Jons muttered, and Ava hated him. The man had been a believer when they started, had come to the mission at almost the exact same time she had come, only the work had soured him spiritually; on the day he announced himself to her as a newly-minted atheist, Ava chilled inside. Only they needed his expertise, and he seemed entirely willing to stay on even after his fall—in a perverse way, even more so. *My ethics, and my humanity, are entirely the same, Ava. Only without the middleman.*

She looked down at the boy's right hand and it was clenched tightly in a fist.

"Better run some morphine into him overnight, give him a drip," Jons said. "Look into some antibiotics too—what do we have still...?"

Ava managed to pry the fingers open just a little, and when she had two of them away from the palm she knew why she had loved him, her flash-loving, even the first moment he came in: there was a small crucifix in the hand attached to a miniature rosary string. She let the fingers go and the boy closed the fist tight, tight again, and Jons was there so she couldn't say anything to him but she closed her own fingers around the boy's to get the message into him that she too was one of the ones who held fast to God.

□   □   □

The next day a number of people came in who had low-level infections from someone in St. Marc who was performing tattoo services. Whoever it was, he or she had been using an unclean needle and ashes to make the good luck designs and was probably transmitting blood at the same time. The marking she saw on two of the mildly sick people's arms were vodou insignias plus commercial names from American products: *Kamel* and *Pepsi* in swirling fashionable letters.

"Get somebody who isn't doing anything to go down to the village and see if it's that *houngan,*" Jons said at the afternoon gathering. He was wearing a shirt with many pockets and took a cigarette out of one of them, a clear violation of procedure on which no one called him. They had had trouble with a particular leaf doctor before, one who was opposed to everything they did because it was *blan,* the same *houngan* who used to come into the mission compound at night and urinate in the clean water holders so they would have to dump them all and resterilize the tanks. "If he's using a hypodermic we've got a problem."

After that they had only to run through status reports on who had yellow fever, septicemia, of course malaria; and then the chapel prayer after labors, which Jons no longer attended. By evening most went back to their rooms or out onto the low balcony that looked across the outdoor showers and then up north toward Bombardopolis. The nurses and doctors and some of the social workers would gather there most nights to watch the sun wash down across the sea and talk knowingly about American interventionism. It was always divided between the people who wanted America to annex the island altogether, make it a protectorate at least but preferably an unsung colony like Puerto Rico, which would allow for a modicum of humanitarian aid; and those who believed the island was already an undeclared colony, that the military and the Macoutists were in constant alliance with certain unstated elements in the U.S. who ran drugs into Florida for them on the promise that Haiti would remain an import economy. Maintaining an unstable government in the third world when it is linked to economic activity is a very productive strategy. You never let it fall completely, lest somebody rebuild it the way Castro did, off the monetary grid; but neither do you let it stand, lest it demand a living wage and enter into something like a true free market, of which U.S. world trade certainly was not one. Ava had heard it all before, for years now. At one time she had felt the same fresh thrill, the same lucent possibility for change. Now it seemed only the young voices of the enthusiasts changed, growing jaded and silent, arriving fresh and anticipatory the next rainy season to take up the battle again. She went to her own room and slept before she was aware of trying.

□   □   □

The boy was lying in almost the same position in which they had left him, although the sweaty tousle of sheets suggested that he had been moving around, perhaps in a fever. Ava checked his forehead, touching at the swollen stiffening skin around the mask of bandages as gently as she could: yes, he was definitely feverish, but most of that was probably an initial reaction to the assault. There were myriad battles going on inside this body, and they would take their toll.

She worked with the mantles on a cot-side lamp until she could get it to ignite and then brought in a pewter bowl and soaps from the front room. The boy's shoulders were already looking better; he had a body that was young and finely built, structured like a functional machine, which gave promise that the healing would be fast. There were going to be scars: that much could not be avoided, not with conditions the way they were. For a moment something inside her ached for a world in which scars remained, and her hand stayed motionless with the dripping cool water over his stomach. How thin her own wrists had become across the years, how lean and graceless the fingers! She had hardly even noticed the change, and now the skin on her hands was dry and tough, the bones seemingly elongated, like the hand on an aged woman. But she prayed, she prayed over the silent figure then that they could at least save the eyes.

When the sponge-bath was finished she checked the IV drip at both ends, lifting the plastic bags a little to make sure it had no clogs, and it was only when she had changed the sheets underneath him that she seemed to realize for the first time the nakedness of the body in the cot. Ava marveled to herself on how fine a face it was that lay half-concealed under the gauze and medical salve with its peculiar vinegary smell, how every part of him fit cleanly and in order with every part. To her suddenly the broken body of this nameless not-yet-a-man from somewhere in St. Marc was all at once a masterful whole, an artwork of stunning proportion. She wanted with a new and almost trembling force to touch him again along the lean muscles and bones, to touch him not with a sponge and a cloth but with only her fingers, to sense the physical person of him in a way that she already knew would be like touching the wind.

Strangely, she wept a little, and, not knowing precisely why she had done this, left the curtained area and busied herself for an hour with mosquito-netting the momentarily unused cots where they had become torn and other things that needed doing around the ward. The night air outside the windows was warm and fragrant with the blush of tropical vegetation. When a lay orderly with dense scholarly glasses asked her if she fancied some star gazing she was ashamed of her lightheadedness.

On her way out she entered the boy's tent again and pulled up a small stool by the cot-side and asked him in the best Creole she could if there were anything she could do for his comfort. Since he refused to eat or drink, Jons and a French doctor named Mailloux had suggested they arrange a second IV drip directly to the stomach for nutrient, but that could not be put in place for another twenty-four hours because it would all just come back up again until the morphine had had time to set. But had she not heard him, just then, whispering something soft and promising from out of his sleep, just as she was leaving the room? Now the boy said nothing once more, shifting only slightly in his awkward bed and seeming to listen. After a minute she checked his right hand again: it was still clenched and for a moment she thought she saw the fingers work back and forth just slightly over the wooden face of the crucifix that was so small she could not even find it. She put her hand on his again and she prayed for him, she prayed to St. Theresa of the Missions and to Mary the Blessed Virgin and comforter to the sick, and she leaned down and spoke quietly into the boy's ear to let him know he was safe now, she was there, with him always.

□   □   □

By late in the afternoon the boy was not showing signs of improving. The drugs they used had come through in a group package over a month before and no one was really certain how well they had kept inside the refrigerators. Jons and Dr. Mailloux had him moved to secondary space they had cleared off of the main infirmary to get him away from possible contagion: there were still three malarial cases on the hall that were in the strongest part of their downward curve. Everyone in the mission had contracted malaria at least once, including Ava, but any kind of blood-related infection could be dangerous. When next she passed by his cot she saw the second stomach IV had been put in, its colored tube coiling downward into his person like an accusation.

That night she went early from the dining tables and began her prayers in the chapel. She prayed again to the Virgin Mother of Christ, to whom she had always felt a closeness, even in the days when she was new on the island and everything was frightful to her. At that time the Blessed Mother had comforted her more than once: she believed she had felt the sudden and ineffable presence of warmth passing through her from a source deeper and more lasting than any self. Once it came when she was assisting in the opening of a patient's chest, and she saw the red vena cava surrounding the heart jumping and alive on one side like a frog in a thin sack and the sight was almost too much for her, the sight of the source of life in the body exposed before imperfect eyes was almost too great, but the sudden warmth and assurance had come instead and she performed her small duty without having to step down.

Now she prayed to the Virgin with fervor, she prayed to her sinfully not only for the soul but for the body of the young boy lying in the newly-cleared back room, his stomach and arms sprouting plastic tubing like some strange tropical vine. She prayed for his body to be made well and for those hidden eyes to be preserved still under the swelling; she prayed for the antibiotic shipped in from Ft. Lauderdale to be not denatured in the long wait; she prayed for the water they were using in cutting the morphine into solution to have no parasites in it and not to have been contaminated by the *houngan*. More than she had prayed even for the other patients, the ones who were in her prayers every night individually when they first came in and then in a mass as their faces and conditions drifted together for her like anonymous sand, she prayed for him on account of his strength and the devotion he showed to Christ in a land of vodou and decay. And at the close of her prayers she raised her fingers to her face to wipe away tears and there were no tears at all but she found the contour of skin over bone there strange to her, like touching another person.

□   □   □

At midnight Ava went down again into the infirmary. There were some locals sleeping outside on the ground whom they had not been able to drive away from the compound; but Jons and some of the others had decided to allow them to stay as long as they were apart from the sickrooms. One of them watched her going in without speaking, a thin quizzical expression in the dim.

She saw it almost as soon as she had pulled the sheet-curtains back and worked the mantles on the cot-side lamp: small and ineffectual on the dusky tiles, its trail of string wrapped around it like an afterthought. With an audible gasp Ava stooped and lifted the crucifix from the floor and kissed it and kissed the hand it had dropped from. She placed the crucifix back in the boy's hanging palm, unsleeping as she had known he would be, she placed it back in the center of his loose hand where he had gripped it so hard that the side had dug into his skin at places and left little red angles. She held onto the hand and she spoke to the boy in the unreal world of the infirmary, just the two of them in the oval of hissing mantled light, and she told him no, not to do it, not to give up on Christ. She told him she knew about the days which came to all believers that cast them into doubt. She knew about the pains of this life, of this world which seems to be the whole world but is only a speck in the great opening pupil of creation; that she knew the feeling of loss when it becomes too great for the small, battered soul to understand. She told him of the life she had known in America, the farmhouse where her family had lived for three generations and her father's unkind eyes; of her struggles to become educated when it was believed she was slow, and the great fear she had never told of how she might in the end fail at all she tried to accomplish. Of her mother's death and the moment when they had sat staring face to face after she had been called home to the dying-bed and she realized the delirious old woman had forgotten her, simply lost hold of the memory of who her own daughter was like something of insignificance. She pulled the loose, unresisting fingers over the crucifix again and she whispered to him to hold on, hold onto this one ship for life, this was the only ship that was sailing the way toward harbor and boon.

But the hand felt what she was placing in its palm and threw the thing down again, it threw the crucifix away from the body as if the hand were not one with the body, as if it were a separate and an evil entity opposed to the body that had willed itself so strongly to grasp on to the bark of life. She stooped and grabbed up the wooden piece with its little string and tried to place it in the hand again but the boy rose and pushed her away. He turned fiercely on his side now, so that his gauzed and battered face was turned away from the lamp and away from her, the salves dripping in thin lines from his face like tears; only then it occurred to her that the light might have been hurting him, that as the swelling finally came down the healing eyes might need to be shaded from such direct stimulation. Frantically she burned her fingers as she turned down all the mantles and together they sat in the darkness, hearing the occasional sound of somnolence from another bed or the clink of an IV pole tied to some fitful sleeper. The injured were sleeping their restless sleep around them and they two were alone, and with no sound in the trees outside and in the blankness she tried to understand what his world was, she tried to know him and she tried to hold his hand.

□ □ □

Fr. Cassian stopped her in the garden the next day.

"Is it something spiritual, Ava?" he said.

No, she told him, and she must have smiled convincingly because he returned the smile like a small gift they had passed from one to another. She told him it was just the work, that it was hard work they had chosen to do here even if it was God's work, even if it was holy and work for which they had been chosen. Still it had a way of tiring. She almost laughed a little.

"You've not been crying?"

It was nothing, she assured him, even taking the rough skin of his hand in her own, in which there was no feeling. The old man leaned over to her ear.

"I can no longer sleep," he whispered, touching at her hair with an unexpected tenderness.

At the end of the hour she was making her way past the back gates when Jons saw her through a window. He motioned several times and then came hurrying out, his form split apart by the shadows under the palms. The heat of midday was bringing out flies.

"I have something... it's the sack fellow," he said awkwardly. Suddenly to Ava his red hair and the long flat line of beard he kept looked out of place in the gigantic sun and the Caribbean air: his light-squinted eyes were exceedingly pale, a blue so faint they looked to her like pieces of the sky, receding into an impersonal light and almost disappearing.

"I know," Ava said. Her voice, it seemed to her, came with courage; it felt warm and relaxed to her ear. "I have been asking for the wrong thing, Mr. Kroner. The fault was mine."

"Ava..."

"I know you don't believe that, you don't believe in efforts of the spirit as well as of the body. But that doesn't really matter. All last night I stayed in the chapel, Jons, and through prayer I have been prepared for the Lord's will. I know the boy has taken a turn for the worse. Infection has set in. Dr. Mailloux is going to have to operate through the inflammation. It will be disfiguring."

Jons watched her for a moment and the copy of the paper he had been using to rock the hot, still air gently in one hand stopped moving. He looked at her with something in his expression she hadn't ever seen before.

Why, he's in love with me, Ava thought, suddenly. *The poor man loves me desperately.*

"It isn't the beauty of the face that matters," she said now clearly, without shame, not with vanity but with a justifiable pride; and to her own ear again the words had the amusing clarity of conviction. She smiled on the sad face of this large European man, this sad man made of many despairs, this seed thrown on difficult ground who had not found the faith or the resolution to persevere. She looked at him and when she tried to read his expression she felt herself full of cool and lifting air.

"I'm not sure what you're trying to say, Ava," Jons answered at length. "I was going to tell you that the boy's fever broke some time last night. I would have called you but you weren't in your room... in fact, he seems finally to be getting better. For a while, I'll admit, I didn't think... because he was acting like he was in shock since he came in..."

"Since he came in," Ava said. It had sounded so final, the way he said that. And she wanted to hand all that finality back to the man, place all that finality back in his lap like a big sack of something unusable, something for which she had no use and which in her own ethic had no place. She wanted to say all these things about the so-called altruism and so-called love that would make a declared atheist want to stay on working at a hospice of Christ, and his defeatism and the secularism that colored and shamed his approach. She wanted it all to come across just in her look.

"Anyway," he went on slowly, "the worst seems to have passed. We released some fluid pus this morning and the swelling has gone down enough that we were finally able to pry open the area around the eyes to see if they'd need to do some recuperation work. Not that there's anybody here who's trained enough to do that, but... well. As it turns out."

He looked closely at her again for a minute and she did not say anything in return. How bold she felt!

"Ava, he hasn't got any eyes at all," Jons said. "They're thinking it may not even have been Uncle Sack, but some underground organ people... selling these things on a black market..."

Ava smiled. His love was simply flowing out of him now, the foolish man! She could see it marked all across his features, she giggled because he was so boyish, so like an awkward boy on a first date, one she needed to mother and make calm. He would always need her here, always, to mother him like a foolish boy and make him feel wanted. But how he positively trembled for her! How his face opened like a flower!

Dyebon

There was a noise in the street. The beggars wanted him to come over and see something, but they were crowded around so closely with their cans and tinfoil plates that for a minute he couldn't get through. Then the little group opened up and he could see it: a man crouched on a small wooden platform with wheels, something that looked like it might at one point have been part of an orange crate. The man was thin. All the beggars in the countryside were thin; thinner and more in need than he had seen anywhere else in the world, and in his younger years at least the Archdiocese had kept him moving. The island had been his third major assignment. After the first two a fellow Jesuit in Baltimore had confessed that there was still a rather nineteenth-century fear among the higher orders that if missionaries settled for too long in any one population there was a danger of them "going over," becoming more native in their thinking and less emblems and organs of Christ. It had happened before.

This beggar wore a checkered shirt and even one of those status-symbol watches that looked like they belonged on a middle-class man, but his pants were filthy—so filthy and crusted to the skin that Fr. Cassian wondered if they were ever changed. Underneath them the legs were thin, but they seemed to be alive;

the musculature was still apparent and he did not recognize at first glance the telltale signs of atrophy. But the man held his bone-legs out stiff in front of himself like an offering, like something he was trying to hand over to the *blan* priest and have him inspect. The little crowd pointed at them over and over again and kept saying something, but his Creole was weaker than his French and he did not understand.

"*Paralysie?*" he asked of the boy who was his interpreter and who worked five days a week at the mission in St. Marc, translating the gospel for locals during services. "Was he shot? Beaten by police?"

The boy said he did not know. He was listening to the beggars all talking at once, and seemed to be understanding them but then not understanding. The boy was a recognizable mulatto, and was well-educated and looked well-educated, and perhaps for these reasons the beggars were not eager to communicate with him. There was always the color tension: When a Haitian bishop had come to see Fr. Cassian at the mission once about an ecumenical project, he had flatly refused to speak through the boy, insisting on a second interpreter who only repeated his Creole verbatim to the boy, who then translated it for the priests. Fr. Cassian knelt down in the dust next to the crippled man.

"*Qu'est-ce qui se passe avec toi?*" he asked slowly, looking into the rheumy, unclean eyes, even the white rims of which were unclean. He could smell the man, just as he could smell Titanyen all around him, and always for a day or so after coming here: rotten tobacco piles and fish, mango pits, animal hides. The hands of the people around them were tapping at his shoulders and gesturing toward the legs.

He had decided simply to give a blessing when the crippled man reached out and took his two fingers, forcing them down onto his broken feet. There was a reaction from the crowd. Fr.

Cassian hesitated for a moment while something rippled through his body, some instinctive revulsion; and then he gripped the feet well in his broad, strong hands, feet whose skin had the hard consistency of cardboard. He knew these men slept in the streets at night, when the military or someone else did not drive them out; and when they were driven out, they slept in sheds and unlocked cars and sometimes even in the caves. He looked at the bare, ruined feet in his palms. In the center of each was a heavy piercemark, running completely through to the sole. The bent toes themselves seemed to have twisted up a little around these insults; they would never stand again.

"Did Macoute do this to you?" he asked the man, the hollow tension, the revulsion in his chest rising. He hated his own disgust, and yet it was absolute, intractable. *"L'Armée?* Who shot through the bones so you would not be able to walk?"

But the man kept asking with his mute, expectant eyes and the other beggars kept tapping in a flurry at Fr. Cassian's shoulders and pointing to the wounds. In a minute the boy nudged his way back into the circle.

"Now I got it," he said in the colloquial English he had learned from American instructors. "People come here ten, fifteen years ago, doing a big conversion, big sweep." He said a Creole word.

"Baptists."

"Okay, sure. *Ale* Satan, everybody gets to be *Chrétien.* The town starts a festival. *Pak,* Easter Day, big show. This man, he had money and a house, chickens and money, before the festival. He comes from a family of *madan-sara,* big sellers of things. But at festival time, okay—he feels a call. You know." The boy held one hand softly up to his heart and gestured with the other toward the cloudy sky. "A call."

"I understand."

"And, okay, so he volunteers to be the *Dyebon.*"

"The *Dyebon?*"

"Someone gets up on the... you see..." the boy started drawing it in the dust with his finger.

"The cross," Fr. Cassian said. "Someone plays Christ in the festival. And they build a cross and parade him through town."

"Wi," the boy said, sitting back now that his meaning had been understood. "He held on with his hands," he added, as if to qualify something.

The beggars watched in silence, their faces expectant. Metallic-green flies were crawling on the man's feet and no one made an effort to shoo them away.

"He sleeps on a mat now," the boy said after a minute, when it became apparent the priest was not going to speak. "He's very proud, okay. A real hero."

Fr. Cassian looked at the ruined flesh he was barely touching and began to rub its contours in tiny, hesitant motions in his hands. Though he knew they were mute and unfeeling some deep part of him was afraid of the feet, afraid lest they should crisp and spark up into flame under his coarse, stupid flesh. Suddenly he felt the feet larger than himself, of greater import than even his decades of work in exotic unloved countries of the world, of which he was so vain; they seemed knitted of a moment and a presence that threatened to weigh through him and the mission and weigh through the round dusty earth itself. The crippled man's twin ugly eyes watched him with that eager look, that questioning that needed to be understood. He could smell the crowd.

"What should I tell him you say?" the mulatto boy asked, already uninterested. He did not like the sights of Titanyen or these men; he wanted to go back to the mission and eat dinner, and from there to his own family. His father was a merchant and came home from the markets in the evening.

"Tell him not in all Jerusalem have I found such faith," Fr. Cassian said. "Tell him I said that."

"Sure, but I don't know," the boy answered, slapping the dust off his pants as he stood. "I don't know if that translates so good."

Onde

First came the coffin: two men on the left side and two right, carrying it high and balanced with the same dexterous skill the workers showed in tipping baskets of mangoes and bright green oranges and even coconut halves on their heads, the lacquered wood of the thing seeming to hang dire and contentless between hands. Behind it trailed a small crowd of women, empty palms raised theatrically to the air as they passed, grasping nothing, and their voices, at times like a single broad lament, lifted against the already deepening sky. The mourners processed from the little squat church with its bell tower, unusual for this town where lofts in which men with rifles could hide had been systematically torn down a generation before; and out through the marketplace, where sellers from Kenskoff paused and watched the floating bark and crossed themselves and spat over their elbows to ward off the Evil Eye. Some joined in with individual cries, others not looking up in their hurry but whooping toward the dusty ground as they fitted plantain and breadfruit and string-tied corn back into lidless boxes. The procession passed down the street, curving away toward the trees.

After it was gone Thomas LeFay went and stood once more at

the edge of the walkway. As he paused his fingers worked themselves into the back pockets of his jeans, a mannerism that—had it
not been for the white skin, the sandy-blonde hair that midway
into life still came in a full and almost effeminate flop, the belt
straps full of his money and film—would immediately have
labeled him as an American. Across the water clouds were drawing
together, a storm bulk being fashioned with surprising rapidity.

"Going to be something?" the *Royal* asked, coming up alongside LeFay from a battered palm trunk where he had been taking
his lunch. "Hand of God?"

"Hard to say," LeFay answered, watching the banks deepen
and spin, as if turned by unseen hands. The fishing skiffs were all
dropping sail or making for harbor like black wedges against the
suddenly chopping gray, their owners stepping over the sides into
the water and tying the prows to pierwood and mangrove roots in
an easy, practiced motion. "From the colors up there I'd say we're
going to see some trouble. How much, though, you can't really
say until it hits."

"All manner of warning noises on the radio," the *Royal* said,
gesturing with his handheld transistor. "Small craft warning, large
craft warning. As if there were anything on the island other than
small craft. They keep saying *onde, onde.*"

"Tropical storm," LeFay said. *"Onde tropicale.* That means it's
going to be big."

He had come to this part of town before, once, in the days
when *dechoukaj* was something you did to trees, not a real political possibility. It had been a quick jaunt, into the economic slum-
land of the West and back out again, with only one trip to a
mission-staffed infirmary after swallowing some ice out of a hotel
machine ("Damned lucky you didn't take it into your head to try
the university hospital on Guilloux," the medic on charge had
said, "or you might not ever leave.") and a lot of pictures of

excited ex-Zinglins wearing those characteristic Rolex gold-plates and smiling for the Nikons. It was the reason he had been picked as the ablest-bodied man for peeking in on the American third world this time around, with Baby Doc teetering and Aristide making waves, and those same Rolex watches on the same young-faced men who were no longer smiling for cameras now that they had tasted blood. That had been a reason to come back and some days, maybe even most days, waking up in his hotel room on the Brian Wilson floor where he never swallowed the ice, he persuaded himself it was his real reason.

"Breathe in the air now," LeFay said. "You can taste it."

"Bloody Christ," the *Royal* responded, without heat. "Damned if you can't. It tastes like... has a twinge to it, doesn't it? Something like..."

"Lemons."

"Something like," the *Royal* assented, looking upward at LeFay from under the wide-rimmed Panama that singled him out not only as British but as *neg sot*, a purely Haitian term that LeFay sometimes thought was invented for such people. Not that he had any animosity toward the *Royal*—they had exchanged tedious pleasantries again when they passed quite by accident, and he and LeFay had a drink together at San Martin. The *Royal* was a short-ish, puffy-faced man with a haze of sweat that glittered on his cheeks; he wore the Panama everywhere and starched shirts and pants he evidently ironed in his hotel room. During their small lunch together he spoke at some length on what was apparently his favorite subject, the effect of subconscious guilt experienced by the French in Haiti, likening it to the dutiful yearly visit of a divorced parent to a recidivist child. "After they ran up the body of Henry Christophe, what was there to come back to? It's only a national complex now that needs occasional hot-rubbing with charitable works." The day after their conversation the table at

which they sat was shattered by crossfire, its glass top blown to
pieces and the wood underneath it punctured in one spot by
four neat holes into which LeFay, passing again by chance, slid his
fingers.

"That's electricity in the air, when you smell lemons. You
don't get that in the States unless you live along the Gulf of
Mexico. Look there."

In the graying distance a single and then a second lance of
clean light descended onto the tree-filled top of Ile de la Gonave.
Where the rain was already falling out across the water a vague,
sheet-like discoloration of the air was visible, something solid but
tenuous moving inland in one hastening body. Behind them the
market had wholly vanished, the last few sellers returning at a run
to grab up sacks of rice and lamp oil and oatmeal mix that they or
someone else had left and transport them to whatever places they
were disappearing into among the streets. Across the water the
first thunder came, a distant cannonade.

"Hadn't we better think of debarking?" asked the *Royal,* not
waiting for a response. The white dust that had moments before
been an open selling ground was beginning to be marked with fat
dimes of rain. LeFay pulled the collar of his shirt up across the
sunburn that never left his neck and followed, jogging now
against finger-wide touches of water that were falling out of a still
technically unclouded sky because these were only the out-flung
edges of the storm being cast up on land. The normally blistering
air was actually running cold now, and as they mounted the broad
steps to the church it was something else as well: LeFay noticed
the change before he realized he had already processed this as
something about which he had been warned twice now at the
Washington Post briefings but which he had never actually
believed.

"Look at that," he said, taking the *Royal* by the arm and

breaking his red-cheeked stride. "Son of a bitch. It's going green. The air is going green."

"I do hope you aren't…"

"Son of a bitch," LeFay said. "Look out over the island. They were right."

The sky over la Gonave was the color of a blood-bruise, changing fast, as if there were two skies being viewed through a combined lens. The *Royal* began pounding on the fat wood of the door with one hand.

"Let us in!" he cried, histrionic into the wind that was mounting around them like a wakening presence. "We demand sanctuary! May our sins be forgiven us in this world and the next!"

Someone called something back from the other side of the door and LeFay leaned closer to it and shouted *"Journaliste! Nous sommes avec…"* and the rain passed onto them in a solid wall of spattering lines that made him cry out with the sudden iciness striking him across his back and shoulders like blows from a precise whip. The door opened and they crushed into a shadowy hallway with arched ship-supports for a roof, the walls lined with people, and the little priest in the gray robe closed the door again quickly and locked it against the wind.

"Grammet-la avek nou," the priest said. He was very dark-skinned and healthy looking, although thin, with alert careful eyes, and LeFay wondered fleetingly if he could be *prêtre macoute*—a priest involved in politics on more than a spiritual basis, receiving more than the ascetic's share of recompense.

"E avek oumenm tou," he answered, and the little man smiled. He embraced LeFay quickly and then the *Royal* as well, patting their sides as he did so and once along the hips.

"Looking for weapons," LeFay said in English. "Are you carrying?"

"God, no," the *Royal* said, and the priest disappeared, moving into the back rooms with an alacrity that showed how well the crowd knew him, parting slightly at his presence. LeFay started inching back through the hall, feeling the eyes on him and his whiteness, his otherness. He felt the gaze on his camera and everything positive and negative it could mean in a country where the outside news was alternately a vehicle of resistance and, when no change came, a symbol of the greater world's indifference. He felt the fingers of children trying to fish in his pockets and did not bother to push them away.

There was a somewhat larger room beyond the hall that was evidently used for saying Mass, equally crowded, with people leaned up against and some even sitting on a makeshift altar. On the wall a stained-glass window depicted a black Jesus gesturing toward cloudy heaven, light making its way down through the tumult to His peacefully upturned face. And the faces of the others watched him here as well: a woman who was holding an infant naked in her arms and trying to breastfeed it; two younger men who had found an empty space and picked plaster off one pinkish wall with an affected indifference that LeFay thought could have belonged to young men anywhere in the world. What appeared to be a husband and wife had brought two crates with them into the church and now held the top down on a group of chickens that wrangled under the wood, dry wings snapping. LeFay made it to a grill-covered front window just as a smack of lightning killed the electric power. The room gave a small cheer.

Outside rain was exploding like tiny shells across the abandoned street, the few stalls that had not been dismantled battering the drops back upward again and their wooden sides running black. One man was still gathering something up off the road, his shirt like a wing above his head, and then he was gone and even twenty feet away became obscure, the sound of the water on the metal roof redoubling. LeFay crouched by a red angle of glass and had the sense that the little church was not a shelter from this rain so much as a moving vessel in which they all were riding, he and the human-scented room. Through the higher window he could see the upper half of la Gonave lost in rain haze and occasional lightning illuminating the palm fronds where they tangled along the water's edge like swimmer's hair.

A child ran out into the road wrapped in a plastic tarpaulin, drops clattering off its surface: when the wind drove a rain gust almost horizontally across the ground the tarp came loose and the boy was revealed naked underneath it, holding to the plastic with both hands like a sail and shouting into the storm. People around LeFay hooted and rapped on the glass, and the boy shook his tiny genitals at them in a crazy comic gesture and ran. LeFay watched the tarp banging and rolling in the other direction down the street, folded and unfolded by the wind.

"Listen to that," a voice said at his side. It was the little priest in the gray cassock, a wooden cross now visible hanging down in front from an elastic string. *"That* is power."

"You speak English?" LeFay answered, realizing the fatuousness of the question even as he finished it.

"Un peu," the priest grinned, ambiguous. "With German I am not so good, with French fine, English a little better."

"You're a scholar."

Again the ambiguous nod, half self-deprecation, half acceding. "Only one has to do what one can here. As much as one can. It is a duty for the upper class to achieve scholarship equal to the American upper class. Is this correct?"

"The language, or the sentiment?" LeFay said, but the little priest seemed not to have understood. "Your English is fine," he added.

"You are a newspaper fellow? From America, I see."

"I am, yes. Photographer."

"Going to write a book on Haiti? On the political climate?"

"Diaspora, actually."

"The..."

"Everyone leaving. The people."

LeFay noticed the man's English skills seemed to center around terms such as *political climate;* again he wondered if this church were a center of "dialectics," or the old-time "noirisme," or some other passion politics.

"Well," he tried again. "Just getting a sense of the country."

The priest smiled at LeFay's own ambiguity and for the moment LeFay felt they had reached some cautious détente. The thunder came again, its vibration palpable through the wooden window frame against which his hands rested, and the little priest gestured toward it with his head.

"That sound you hear is Agwe," he said. "She is angry with the land. Agwe is angry with the land because the land is being fed on pestilence. Her rage is justified. But she is also the sound of our new life. You understand? The anger and the conflagration are also the sound of a new life. Say that in the American papers. Tell them that."

"I'm sure they'll appreciate..."

"Tell them Haiti is ready to be born," the little priest said, something in his face sharp now with an aspect LeFay had not seen before, something like the willful energy of prophets. "And not as a puppet to left or to right, to north or to south. On our own power, we will rise."

Thunder toppled over the building's roof and as the tightly-packed room cheered, loudly this time, the little man smiled back at them, as if it were his doing.

"Tell them that she roars to be born again," he said to LeFay. "To the new life."

□   □   □

The *Royal* was standing out in the street.

"Bloody downpour," he said. "Bloody *onde tropicale,* if you have to know." He waved the long narrow antenna from his transistor out across the water and then across town like a prospector seeking gold, but was met with only a silver-gray hiss in all directions. "Surprised it didn't bring the bloody church down around our feet like the wrath of the almighty. Driving?"

LeFay held onto the doorless side of the jeep while it whined and rumbled across the pitted streets and the *Royal* sought solid purchase. The rain had left a long and moving stream of unchanneled water passing down the footpaths, carrying with it a flood's worth of detritus: cardboard boxes in which, perhaps, some had been living or at least sleeping; dozens of rotten fruits and husked shells, the brightly colored and unusable trash that was a hallmark of American trade. Brand names like Mister Coffee and Jordache and PepsiCo making their way trudgingly past. Farther outside of town the long, arcing streams were even stronger, and the jeep had to go slowly in places to prevent the soiled water from foaming up around their ankles. Between two ancient pines the crumpled skin of a steer loitered, trapped by the flow. Most of its head was still attached.

"Merciful God," the *Royal* muttered, working the gears.

They drove until LeFay leaned out of his side of the cab, then wrapped one wrist around the roll-bar for support and leaned farther out.

"Stop here," he said.

In the evening gloom beyond a thicket of trees torches were burning, the oil spitting and running down into the grass from their rounded sides. A small crowd had gathered by the water, and there was some shouting that didn't sound to LeFay like the histrionics of political demonstrations, even the legitimate ones.

It sounded meaner than that.

"Cock fight?" the *Royal* said. "Ceremony?"

"No."

"That's the cemetery, isn't it?"

He stopped the jeep on solid road but left the motor running, and LeFay climbed out and made his way through the trees. The light was bad and he didn't want to risk a snapshot with a flash, not before knowing what he was looking at. He came to the back end of the crowd, where men in shirt sleeves and formal clothes alike were watching something in the middle of the street, raising their hands occasionally and shouting at it, as if their voices were stones they were casting into the fray.

At the center of the crowd was a section of cemetery wall that had collapsed; loose rainwater and pebbles still buckled over its top and through a dozen holes in the poor construction. Black earth had flowed freely into sandy gray and whole sections of the hilly burying place were sluicing off down a series of sharp dropoffs. LeFay guessed it before he actually saw it: There were bodies, two of them visible from where he stood, uncovered except in a gross cloth of dirt and thick rot, lying in the burbling steams as if urging themselves back toward the sea.

"What the devil...?"

"He resold the coffins," LeFay said to the *Royal*, who was looking furtively back through the trees as if seeing the jeep guaranteed it as a possible means of escape. "Probably started by taking off the brass handles at night. There's money in it since the boycott. Eventually he must have gotten around to reusing the whole thing."

"Bloody grave robber," the *Royal* said. "Taking from his own table. Looks like he's got some answering to do."

"Looks like it," LeFay said, seeing the four men who had been coffin bearers at the front of the funeral party push the one who was evidently the undertaker down onto his knees in the wet soil and begin kicking him. *They will probably kill him,* he thought. *They will probably beat him to death right here and now, and bury him without any wood house around him either. An Old Testament kind of justice.* As he watched, the undertaker raised his empty hands imploringly to the crowd, swinging them around as if offering some unseen thing to anyone who might recognize it. Someone knocked him back down, gave a kick to the head.

"Do we intervene?" the *Royal* asked, wincing.

"No," LeFay said, knowing that if he could dream he would dream that night of the bodies of dead men inching their way toward the sea. "No, we don't." He started walking back toward the trees where the jeep lights were running low.

The Blessed

She was standing next to and a little behind the mapou with its sky-spreading limbs. Dieuseul sat down a short ways away, having thought he was alone and not wanting, now, to be seen. Lunch break was an unstated twenty-five minutes for the darker-skinned, and he had wasted five of them bumming a Marlboro off Pierre Salut, whose uncle worked for the cigarette factory in Les Cayes and who always had more then he could smoke, and for that very reason enjoyed being tightfisted. He smoked the unfiltered roll until it was too small to hold and then ground out the end in his palm, and it was only after a minute of thinking nothing at all that he realized she was standing beside him again.

"It's a beautiful day, isn't it?" she said, in mellifluous Creole. "So *belle.*"

"*Wi,*" Dieuseul assented, not wanting to look up. He was guilty, now, of the bag lunch in front of him, especially of the taster flask of coconut rum he had secreted from out of the display case that it was his task to assemble every morning. With three fingers he crumpled the bag a little around the recognizable colored glass; if he had been seen with it he could say he was just holding this coconut taster for a bit while deciding which selection it went with best. His boss believed that each flavor of rum had a distinct character, an inner spirit, and that success in selling them came from understanding the spirits involved. But she had not seen.

"Such a lovely view from up here on the hill," she went on in a dreamy, confiding muse. She looked out over the sand pines and red, broken hills down toward the business district and the shining water. "The island is beautiful in the afternoons. Everything is so... *belle.*"

Then the sun pierced his eyes and Dieuseul saw how she carried her stomach and knew who the woman was who had been standing by the sacred mapou, as if she had climbed down from its branches, and he dropped his sack of cornmeal with the secret flask and ran, making the sign of the cross on his panting, heaving chest again and again.

□ □ □

"What did she look like?" Jaques Lukol said. His boss was a mulatto, the stony face broad-boned and somewhat resembling worked putty. He wore an expression of dour unappeasement that rarely shifted, except on those unpredictable occasions when he flew into a rage and fired someone. Dieuseul had gotten this job, in fact, as the result of one of Lukol's fits of anger that resulted not only in three men being fired but in a broken flask of rum and a small bloodstain on the floor, over which they laid a carpet. As his mother used to say, it was *a lucky piece of bad luck* for Dieuseul, who had been relieved from several other spots that year and spent a good deal of time not working at all. The word among the bottlers was that Lukol did not do any actual work either in his little wooden office at the back of the plant, because he had relatives who owned the operation and shipped the rum out of Haiti and relabeled it Cuban, and sold it illegally at

American ports to great profit. Oftentimes you saw him sitting behind his big wooden desk with his hands laid flat on a record-keeping book, doing absolutely nothing.

"She was wearing a blue floating robe," Dieuseul said, "as blue as the sky between clouds. And around her feet were clouds she could walk on so she did not have to step on the earth. And I looked in her face and behind her head was a double ring of stars."

As he spoke Lukol's impassive expression grew into something Dieuseul had never quite seen before. There was a group forming behind him now, the sounds of work stopped and the wary eyes and slightly open mouths of four and then eight men waiting on him to continue. As the odors of rum and sawdust mingled in his head Dieuseul realized what he must look like: He had run all the way from the far end of the hill.

"And fire and water," he added a little louder. "And inside her eyes there was fire and water and stars. And voices... people singing."

Lukol continued to peer at him for a moment, his new expression going a little puzzled.

"Voices... in her eyes?"

"Around her, around her head and feet," Dieuseul corrected quickly. "And when she stood next to me I felt... I felt..."

He looked about the room, letting his face relax into a slight smile that forgave even the two men who had found him asleep in the loading room the week before and beaten him for it. "My heart was taken away and replaced with a new one."

There was general assent; someone sighed.

"And her face was black," Dieuseul added, careful not to look at Lukol. "Beautiful all-black skin, like a sky with no moon. And when she spoke to me..."

"The Blessed Mother spoke to you? To *you?*" Lukol cried, his beefy hands starting incredibly up as if to touch Dieuseul's shoulders and then hesitating in the air. It was just a tiny hesitation, the way one would pause before touching some rare and precious item that might fracture at the contact. "What did she say?"

"She said..."

Dieuseul's eyes drifted up among the rafters and cobwebs that ceilinged the entire one-room operation, his attention dallying now among the motes in the sunbeams as if he were not entirely connected to this world. He thought for a moment about saying *the island is so belle,* but some part of him discarded it. "She told me something big. Oh, big. But... she said it has to remain a secret. Only I can know what it is. Until... *the appointed time.*"

That was more or less how it started.

☐ ☐ ☐

After that day Dieuseul began to work a little slower. He came up the hill from Boutilliers to the distillery at a slightly easier pace, enjoying the fragrant morning air and saying *salut* to the beggars and the people out walking dogs. The first day it had just been a little late, four or five minutes, and Lukol had watched him come in not meeting eyes with him or anyone else, and for just a moment he might have said something but then he did not. The second day he was six or seven minutes late, and all day long while he worked, breaking up the glass in the imperfect bottles that came in shipments and removing the paper as best he could and getting the pieces back into the crates to be melted again, Lukol paced in his little back room, looking out at Dieuseul and then pacing some more and saying nothing. On the third day Lukol came over to the cramped desk space where Dieuseul worked.

"This morning," he began. "This morning..."

"*Wi?*" Dieuseul said, raising his face slowly with a mute, kind expression, his eyes drifting with tenderness over his employer's pitted cheeks.

"*De rien,*" Lukol said.

By the end of the day Dieuseul was only down to half the number of bottles in his *finish* crate, with a second crate of unbroken deformities waiting behind that one. It was more than enough, he knew, to have had him fired the week before; there were plenty in town who would take his place for even fewer *gourdes*. But no one mentioned the extra crate of unfinished bottles with their weirdly bent necks, their chipped ends or unhappy sealed mouths. At the end of the day, instead of noticing them, Dieuseul let his gaze drift appreciatively among the light shafts and the motes. Occasionally he hummed.

By the second week there were two crates of unfinished bottles and Lukol was pacing in his office again. He had started to sweat more than he used to, broad circles of perspiration appearing under his arms when he wore gray instead of white, and he passed his hands frequently up and across his half-exposed cranium. He came and stood by Dieuseul's position.

Dieuseul pretended not to see him. When finally he could pretend no longer, he looked up at the boss's face with slow benevolence. The beefy Lukol, he thought, looked very tired.

"It's about the selections for visitors," Lukol managed. Aside from breaking up imperfections, Dieuseul's job was also to change the samples each day, to keep them fresh, and to help distribute capfuls to visitors when visitors came through. It was true, they had not seen many tourists in recent months, the government people were staying away for right now and the missionaries did not drink. Nevertheless this was a part of his job. Had he forgotten?

Dieuseul smiled understandingly; he would remember now.

Lukol cleared his throat. Also he wanted to mention that the cane truck would be coming some time that month and everyone would be required to unload the cane and pile it in the store room until it could be used. Dieuseul knew how heavy the work was and he understood that all the men would be needed. That was not going to be a problem, he hoped.

Dieuseul assented that it was not.

"What did she say to you?" Lukol erupted, as if unable to control the ejaculation. His eyes were red at the rims and locked abruptly on Dieuseul's own, like boring instruments. "When will you tell us?"

Dieuseul paused, as if for a moment he had trouble comprehending what it was the older man could be asking of him. "Oh, *the lady.* She said..."

Dieuseul waited. For just an instant he had heard the clinking of glass in boxes and the scrape of work tools pause, just a beat; just the slightest waiting hold in the steady daily motion of the men all around him. The air was sweet with fragrance.

"No... the time is not yet."

The next day the second and third crates of waiting bottles were gone. Dieuseul pretended not to see.

□ □ □

At the end of the month a woman appeared at the front doors to the distillery, sitting in the greenish predawn air as if she had been there for some time already. The other workers ignored her; they stood by the doors smoking Marlboros they had bought off Pierre Salut and waited for Lukol to show up. When Dieuseul arrived she rose abruptly from her spot and pointed to him.

"You're the one," she said. "You're the one who saw the *lady.*"

Dieuseul stopped in his loping walk. He had been thinking of other things, and this vision of what turned out to be a surprisingly young girl done up in a much older person's dress startled him.

"M'pa Konnen..." he began, and the girl dropped to her knees and grappled his legs with such force he almost fell. The cane shard he had been sucking on dropped into the dust.

"Erzulie!" she cried. *"Stop my bleeding! Erzulie stop my blood!"*

Dieuseul had his hands on the girl's knotty shoulders, stumbling backward to prevent himself from falling; but she followed him with great convulsions of her knees, hobbling across the chalky earth and clutching at his legs with tight sharp fingers. The crazed motion of her legs made loopy dirt ovals on the front of her dress.

"Bless me Mary!" she cried into the settling dawn air. *"Bless me!"*

□   □   □

After that evening, it seemed—later on, Dieuseul was unable to accurately distinguish when things had taken such an abrupt and accelerated turn—people began wanting to touch him. Statuettes of the Virgin appeared on the grass and gravel path leading up to the distillery, along with carefully-plucked flowers wrapped in newspaper. Lukol generally kept the beggars away from his door with a stick, saying they were the *kiss of death* for business, but in the evenings now not only beggars but people from Boutilliers and Barbancourt on the other side had begun to gather in small groups along the path and to light candles and wait for Dieuseul to come walking up or down the hill. As he went by the increasing lines some began to call out to him to remember a son or a husband who was coughing up black; or a spotted swine that was going to die of the fever; or a relative in

America who never sent money. Dieuseul smiled and lifted his hands gently to wave at them and say *salut* or *Bondye Remmen-w.* If Lukol himself was walking at his side—as had now begun to happen more and more frequently—Dieuseul would make a point of stopping and consoling some thin-boned, palsied man who sat on a bananamat begging. Once an elderly woman wrapped in what looked like a burlap sack came from the side of the road and grabbed onto his sleeve, and when Lukol raised his stick to strike Dieuseul told him *No, let her be. You must find peace in your own dwelling.* Lukol hesitated while in his eyes something incredulous glowed, and after a moment the stick came down and disappeared at his side.

Soon there were people in the mornings and the evenings as well, some pressing photographs into his hands and kissing at his fingers as he went by. *This one taken by the Macoute; this one disappeared by the junta. This one went out looking for work; have not heard from him since. Alive or dead? Pray for me.* Slips of paper with names written on them were passed even into his folded arms. Old men who had been sitting cross-legged in the dust since the night before reached out to tap at his feet without comment. Younger men shouted out to him for *borlette* numbers, for protection against AIDS. Dieuseul had to stop taking a break for his lunch. By the time he made it to the base of the hill at day's end and cut into the anonymous streets, his heart was gulping in his chest.

Then one day Lukol came out of his office and called to everyone in the bottle-lines to stop working. His little eyes were wrinkled up and his mouth bent into an angle that, had it been anything other than a strange visitor to his face, might have signified pride. The amount of rum sold had doubled once and was getting close to doubling again. Lukol at first had three people standing out in front of the distillery with the little taster cups

Dieuseul had once managed, but in time he found he was able to charge even for these. White faces had been seen in the little crowds, and it was thought their shop was becoming a special attraction. A magical quality had come to be associated with certain flavors of the rum; some of the people waiting by the long walk up the hill drank the coconut spice and nothing else all day. One man had been seen pouring it carefully across sores on his leg.

Dieuseul no longer worked. Instead he came in to the distillery and sat at his post for hours, not even glancing down at the area where the crate of green and blue bottles had once lived. He drank openly, glutting himself until the hot room swam around his head, then slowing down when even this open display produced no ill effects. The flowers were arriving almost daily, and he fingered their soft unthinking petals. Lukol walked around him from time to time with eager looks, seeming always on the verge of having something to say; but then just raising his hands noncommittally to the air, staring brightly at Dieuseul with a wettish secret grin.

Dieuseul sat at his station and listened to the people outside singing to Erzulie and to Legba. The more rum they purchased, it seemed, the more they were motivated to song. Some had started sleeping in the high grasses by the gravel path now. Lukol was talking of reorganizing the guided walks through the old distillery that had closed down years before. And there were more foreigners outside the building now too; a strikingly out-of-place face here and there, buying little statuettes and paintings from vendors who had started setting up their own shops on flat areas.

Yet Dieuseul was not happy. His body which had first relished the easy hours had begun aching from lack of labor, and he no longer dared to take even an abbreviated walk outside. The others had long since gone about their business without him, sometimes forgetting for whole days at a time that he was sitting at their sides and carrying on conversations of which he was never a part. Before he had been a familiar, though never loved; from time to time, at least, he was part of the after-work gatherings at the prostitutes and casinos in Boutilliers. It was known even then that he had been sneaking rum out of the shelves, and some of the bottlers initially thought he was *mize,* bad luck for working men, but he had at least been among them.

At the end of each day Lukol stepped out the front doors and addressed the people. Would Dieuseul speak tonight? Was the *appointed time* yet come? *No,* he would say, booming his voice out loud in a basso swing from left to right. Erzulie's words were not yet brought to light. But try the papaya spice. Perhaps tomorrow Dieuseul would speak.

And tomorrow was the same: the tapping of his feet as he walked, as if he had become a strange object of attraction or energy; the postcards and photographs; the tiny items, vodou, Christian, merely anonymous, pressed forcibly in his hands and even dropped down his shirt. Once a woman with a pair of scissors clipped off a piece of his sleeve. When he cried out with sudden alarm she stopped and looked amazedly at the corner of her stolen cloth where a drop of blood had marked it. Dieuseul thought she might cry.

□   □   □

Then came the night he found a smashed bottle littering the steps to his little shared house in Boutilliers. The air was scented badly with the sick, sweet fluid, and Dieuseul had to sweep very carefully around the brick to remove all the pieces. The next evening another bottle had been smashed there. He went inside to find his broom and when he came out a white man was standing in the gloom.

"Dieuseul Sali?" the man said.

"*Wi?*" Dieuseul answered. The man stood unmoving in the weird shadows cast down by moon through the lances of palms; in their shifting light his features seemed to scatter and merge.

"I am from Croix-de-Missions," the man said in a studied French. "I know what you have been doing here. I have been *apprised.*"

Dieuseul was silent.

"Do not bother to answer me," the man said, touching slowly the line of a small crucifix that hung from his neck. "Just listen. Such flights of fancy are to be expected from a people... such as yours... a people whose hearts and spirits are still locked in wicked and ignorant ways. The mission understands how these things come about. We do not judge, it is not our business. But I must warn you to desist. To *desist.*"

Dieuseul shifted a little on the step, making glass ends crack under his foot. In the rooms behind him he could hear the two other families with whom he lived making dinner. One woman had a fever and her husband pounded her fiercely on the back when she coughed to give her some relief.

"Such revelations always precede social revolt," the man in the shadows said. "*Revelation* leads to *revolution.* If you do not stop what you have begun, it will end in politics. You understand me? *Politics.*"

"*Wi,*" Dieuseul said.

"Politics are very dangerous here. They are something you cannot understand and should not try to. Others are working with far greater understanding to fashion the future of this people. Do I make myself clear?"

"*Wi,*" Dieuseul said, but the white priest was already walking down the street.

□　□　□

It was not long before he came to feel himself a man in a cage. For some time he tried coming to the distillery without stopping to speak or even notice the people who cried out to catch his eye; it did not work, lending him, he felt, only more an air of mysterious reserve and authority. He tried staying home altogether, sitting an entire day out at his house with bottles of rum he had openly taken, listening to the neighbor's children crying in the next room, pacing his floor and refusing to turn the handle of the doorknob when people knocked. He drank until the room rotated weirdly and he was obliged to lie down.

In the morning he was ill, and the smell of the feverish woman cooking in a grill out front made his insides clench. His bottles were empty, though he did not remember the second or third one, their round ends sweet to his tongue like kisses but offering no relief. Within an hour the knocking had started afresh, but Dieuseul did not answer it. He ate nothing.

On the third day the white and blue flowers had covered over his doorstep, anonymous packages with cards and misspelled letters slid under the crack, sometimes prayers, sometimes ramblings that to him meant nothing. Other men from the distillery came and pounded with the edge of their hands on the window slats, and called to him through the door in half-interested voices. Lukol himself came and offered him money to return, more money than before the changes he would have made in a year. Dieuseul was silent, dreaming.

In the dream the smashed bottles that had been given to him by the *blan* priest were like a chastening sign; their threat loomed large and fertile in his heart. He felt their edges digging into his sides, their pain replacing the hunger, pain and the thirst that was in him always now like a physical touch. Before him stood a crowd, dozens and scores of people reaching out their hands to grasp his hands, reaching up to him as if from some degraded place. He felt the tremendousness of their need. But when he looked more closely he saw they were only a crowd of misshapen glass, demented, deformed, their colorful eyes and mouths pressed shut by the hand of a dumb creator and twinkling blindly in the light.

□   □   □

Though Dieuseul staggered out in the late afternoon he was met almost immediately by the throng, people pushing trinkets and rosaries and tiny amulets at him. Dieuseul took them all, until letters and photos and locks of hair fell from his grasping fingers like overflow chaff. *Ah bon,* he said, accepting an offered flower; *salut,* he said, patting shoulders and arms with the free backs of his hands. Each motion spilled objects: the head off a child's doll, one eye winking; a small shell with someone's face painted on the inside scallop; but the crowd had more. He walked out of Boutilliers and past a stand of brightly sprouting cactus and into the sun, heading for the rising slope that ascended toward the distillery. The crowd came with him. His feet he could feel almost not at all, and it seemed a long time of walking before he realized he had put on no shoes and the skin of his soles was breaking and hurt.

Ah bon, he said to a man who was gesturing to his heart and then strangely to a boy who may have been his son. *Bien sur.* The distillery itself seemed to burn at the hilltop, like something collapsing: He saw it flame like chaff in a high wind. He felt the mounting armful of trinkets was blazing in his hands, he was carrying a flaming load up the hill toward the building that was already alight. And he began to laugh, a laugh that sprouted and grew fantastically from somewhere deep inside him, from under the feet of the deformed glass people; because he was going to cast them all aside, these twisted shapes with their cards and tokens and trinkets. He was going to ascend the hill and scatter their hopes to the sea. He was going to curse them all like a powerful wind and bring the fiasco toppling down. He was going to be free.

Then he saw her. She was seated with a group of women near the bottom of the hill, the grayish sackcloth wrapped around her shoulders and bunching up at her crossed legs. Her face was plain and small, with a tiny scar visible next to the left eye, possibly left from the pox. She had a naked child in her lap, an infant, and even before Dieuseul stopped to look at her carefully he was absolutely certain, though there was no recognition on her face.

Belle, he thought. *Everything is so belle.*

The pregnancy had been difficult; bringing life was always difficult. Pain came with it. Fever came, sometimes, with it, and the woman looked like she had recently survived a long and difficult fever. Her amber skin glowed with residual heat.

She rocked the child a little in her lap and waited while the two friends for whose sake she had evidently come here rushed over and begged at Dieuseul's calves. As he felt the cool touch of lips against his fingers from which the little gifts were dropping he was watching the other woman, whose look moved over him once with a passing interest before she returned to stroking her child's newly-made head. Lukol, who had seen him coming from his place outside the distillery, was almost ridiculous with enthusiasm as he pushed his way down the hill; in a loud, celebratory voice he was accepting offers of money from the people and thanking them all for Dieuseul and urging them to come and drink. He grabbed Dieuseul's arm and led him up with frantic impatience.

When they reached the hilltop Lukol jumped onto a little platform he had had built, grabbing up a microphone that was installed with an amplifier on a wooden rack: *"He is returned!"* he cried. *"He is returned!* Dieuseul has come back to us…"

Dieuseul stepped out from behind him and looked over the crowd, a terrible air blowing through his head. The remainder who had not understood what was happening rose to their feet when they saw him mount the platform, several women dropping onto their faces as if they had been struck. Lukol had his beefy arms up in the air and was dancing openly, swinging his heavy body around with an enormous grin on his face. Dieuseul could smell the drink in him.

"This is how long the lady asked me to wait," Dieuseul said aloud, and there was silence before a shocked kind of ecstasy surged through the crowd. Some of them, seeing the sunset approaching, had already started packing up their sales items and blankets and were in the process of moving back down the hill. Now they began frantically reestablishing shop. From where Dieuseul stood he could see a bright yellow bus and a crowd of people who had been inside it trying once more to disembark. There were also faces that looked calmly at him from the path, white and black; some faces that looked angrily, almost threateningly, and then clearly so; the face, he thought, of perhaps the white priest who had come down out of scattered moonlight. Faces of adulation and opportunity and faces of careful hatred. But everywhere, the one face of expectation. Dieuseul raised his arms.

"Get the hell off," he hissed at Lukol, and the boss stumbled down in a near-fall. Dieuseul faced the crowd.

"This is what the lady said to me," he began into the microphone, and the people moved one notch closer. Lukol forced his way around to the front, his eyes rolling a little disjointedly in his head, and positioning and repositioning his hands as if to restage the event that was about to take place. But Dieuseul was not seeing him.

"The lady is with child," Dieuseul said, to a communal intake of breath. Where he stood the setting sun was in a locked position before him, driven into the sky and immobilized by the broad sweep of his arms. He knew himself to be terrible and high, like the mapou itself. "Erzulie is with child. That child is about to be born. That child is about to be born right here in Haiti. That is my secret."

A quiet twilight wind moved out through the people, disturbing straw hats and dresses, disappearing.

"That child," Dieuseul cried, selecting faces now from the human press like a man with a poker, "that child that is *about* to be born—that child *is* Haiti. That child about to be born *is* Haiti. The child is going to come to this land because the child *is* this land, every part of it, your house and your house and yours..."

The general face showed confusion: his words were white-hot and stunning them, beyond what their ears could assume. But Dieuseul knew the fever. Transformed, he vaulted on.

"That child is on the way here now. He's coming back to the land that belongs to him. That child is on the way and he's going to take possession, over every house and every farm and every pig and chicken. Over every soldier and every *mambo* and every junta man... and every everything else, including you and including me. That's the message she told me. He's on the way. Get to your houses and your fields. He's on the way. Get to your homes and your families. He's on the way. Look out all you people, because that child is on the way."

There was a general delirium of shouting and rushing to get down the hill and toward the yellow bus and the cars and the paths that led back into town by foot. In the down-pouring tide of it Dieuseul himself walked unmolested. Lukol was knocked over in the melee; he began throwing punches with a tall man and both disappeared in the press. Dieuseul did not see them. The gravel path where he stepped was strewn with forgotten walked-on baskets and beads, with dry rice and crucifixes, with pieces of colored paper and plastic flip-sandals. The people were pushing, running, dispersing; he walked calm in the midst of it like a man treading the ocean and his eye fixed on the last edge of the collapsing sun and thinking, *if I wanted to, I could make that dance. I could reach up right now and make that old lady dance right out of her sky.*

Thomas

I waited by myself in one of the corners of the florist's, leaned against a wall with my head resting out on my knees. The sounds of the street rally had been growing louder for much of the afternoon and by the time evening came many of the people who were afraid of a crackdown were taking refuge inside, sitting or standing in uncertain groups. The priests—of whom there turned out to be three from the Salesian order, the same people who had given birth to Aristide and then tried to disown him—were going from person to person and trying to keep everyone calm. I closed my eyes, knowing no dreams would come, but more tired than I could remember having been in a long time.

□ □ □

Thomas.

"Yes," I said.

You asked me once if I was afraid of anything. The answer is yes.

"Yes," I said again.

But I am not afraid of being killed. There are a hundred ways to be killed here, and it happens to these people every day. Every day of their lives they are being killed. Do you see what I am saying? And I have lived with that, with all that, for long enough now that I am no longer afraid of being killed. I have overcome. Being killed was always such a fantastic concept to me, so unreal, so foolish really. Now it is real, and I have overcome it.

"Yes," I said. "The truth is you are very brave. Much more so than I. I am a little in awe of you for that."

The truth is *you* are brave, Thomas LeFay. Extremely so, although you are looking at yourself too closely to see it. You came down here, didn't you?

"I came after you. That was the only real reason I came back. The rest was an excuse."

But you came nonetheless. That took bravery. Courage. *Elan.*

Jason Stuart behind his mahogany desk, telling me I was the best kind of photographer there was. Why is that? I wanted to know. *Because you're hoping to die out there,* he said. *That's why you don't mind getting into the thick of it.*

□　□　□

I was awake. Outside the now-empty building clouds moved in unhurried bands, like a field of wheat that is being plowed by the air, falling naturally into ordered rows. The rally had dissipated without bloodshed, leaving colorful streamers and leaflets scattered in the road. Off to the west I could see that tropical evening air the local painters were so talented at rendering on canvas; last sunlight was there, not like a cry, but simply as a fact.

Diaspora, she smiled, one of the few times it came out spontaneously. *It sounds so Biblical. Did you really think you had to come back to save me? Did you?*

Her face, the first time I saw her: hair shorter, tan not yet permanent, laughing about the ice machine.

If you are not afraid of being killed, what is it you are afraid of? I asked her.

I do not know, she said. But I am terribly afraid. And I will confess that to no one.

Aren't we all? Isn't everyone?

Not like this. With me it is different. It's always there with me. It's walking near me, all the time. Sometimes more than others, but all the time. Always. Ever since I was a girl. Always. Until it finds me.

What about God?

I believe that God is love, she said. I believe that. But He is not going to prevent us from having to wear the cross. He did not prevent it for his own son, and He is not going to prevent it for me. I wouldn't ask it.

But you want to ask it. You want to. That's your sin.

Ava waited a minute before replying, her image drifting back once more into memory. I looked up and there was a man standing on the steps, regarding me suspiciously.

"Taxi," he said. "A face that color, I think you'd better get north of here soon."

One Who Waits

Claron went down to the water and washed his hands in the churning area of tidepool left by the last waves, now moving out quickly again toward an evening sea. In the flat, raised places where the water had already dispersed, a toss of colored crabs was emerging from frothing pockets in the sand; he watched them battle each other with the stupid bravado of armored fighters, their pincers held wide and tipped in that surprising blue. The tidepool had been steaming all day in the sun and after he cleaned off his hands and arms well he stripped naked and slid himself lengthwise entirely into its depth. The stony bottom was hard and cool against his back and there was only enough water to allow him to be almost covered, and he lay and listened to the hissing streams as the pool overflowed from his weight into a dozen gradually-forming channels. When the boisterous crabs ran over his torso with their sharp leg-ends he did not stop them.

After a little while he rose and dressed and, carrying his sandals under one arm, ascended the beach toward the lighted series of shacks. Between some of the shacks clotheslines were strung with white sheets of clothing suspended from them like idealized figures. He was almost to the grassy path that led away from the beaches when he saw the woman standing there.

She was a *blan*, and thin, and wore clothing peculiar for such heat, as if she had just been transported to the island that very moment and were still wandering about in a small daze. She had a large cross-stitched sun hat on and its ends bent a little in the salty evening breeze that was just beginning to mount from the sea. Under one arm she carried a string-wrapped sheaf of printed papers. When she saw him her face fell; she stared for a moment and then, uttering a desperate little cry, hurried away.

□　□　□

Claron made himself a dinner of *biswit* and fried beans and coffee, mixing the coffee grounds with water right in the cup and waiting for it to cool before he could pick it up. He dipped the bread into the beans and chewed it slowly, wiping the bottom of the bowl with the last piece in soft careful strokes. Then he worked the hard outer skin off a mango—difficult—and cut the inner flesh into four pieces and spread them out on the last slice of bread and ate them one at a time. By that time his coffee had cooled and he was able to sip its sharp flavor slowly, holding the cup balanced in both hands.

After the coffee he set the water to boiling again in its pot for the prescribed twenty minutes to kill bacteria and, bringing a candle mounted inside a broken conch, went and settled himself outside. His shack was one of eight, surrounded on three corners by the same tall grasses and cactus that flanked the sand, and with room enough inside for a floor mattress, a little place to read with a glass-encased lamp, a storage closet and the cooking space. It was more room than many he knew in his home village had, where the families slept stacked one on top of another like strips of wood. He remembered the feeling: sweating, slick skin, close.

When an hour had almost passed the eastern sky out over the water had begun to brighten a little he started to feel uncomfortable. It was a sensation he savored often at this time of evening: tense, a strange distress in his muscles and fibers, something mounting and fluid and still uncertain. But it was there, becoming a solid weight inside him that was not the food he had eaten, but something both less and more substantial, something determinative but at times almost light, almost teasing. Many nights when it was still Claron waited for the moon to rise and spent an hour or more under its strong ascending curve, delighting in the bright stillness and purity, almost, of the vision; every night something quickened inside him at this time; but tonight he was anxious. He lighted a cigarette off the conch and smoked it. She was toying with him, he thought; she would not come. He was like an expectant lover, one who waits. Then he saw the first lean curve of her brightness develop itself over the flat sea and the first tracings of her stabbed-out spear being drawn across the far waves, the bright lance she was bringing even now over the waves to him, and he went inside and turned down the lights and blew out even the hurricane lamp. When he returned to his spot she was standing there.

"I wanted to say I'm sorry," she said in English, which he understood but to which he did not respond. After a moment she added, in a voice that seemed to have been practiced over and over again: *"Je voulais dire que je suis très désolée,"* then fell silent.

The night wind stirred the more suitable dress she had apparently found about her legs, making the fabric luminous like a tide pool. *"Je ne savais pas... that is..."*

The woman looked at the ground, as if she had lost something of significance in the twilight earth.

"I didn't know this was the leper beach when I came here," she said. "Do you speak English?"

The second question had been asked of the shell-littered dirt or the night air, and carried the inflection of one who does not expect an answer.

"Yes, I speak some," Claron said. The woman seemed genuinely surprised.

"Oh, thank goodness," she said, starting to come forward in her relief and then checking herself. "They told me you were a school teacher, before... that is..." She paused. "I'm just new at the... that is, I've only just come onto the island with the outreach program, and except for the refresher course I haven't had even French since high school..."

"Who told you?" Claron said. "Who told you about me? And what do you want?"

Again the young woman seemed at a loss. Her face showed pain; she had the attitude of a child standing in front of an angry father from whom some remonstration is due.

"It was terribly rude of me to react the way I did. I know that Jesus stayed with people... people like you... and that it's not your fault, the way... the way you are. I just wanted to say..."

"You go away now," Claron said. *"Ale."*

The *blan* woman stood painfully in the now-pronounced shadows for a time with the spearblades clicking around her, and then turned; or rather the luminous dress turned quietly in the shadows that seemed not to surround it but which it seemed to inhabit, and she was gone back into the grass. Claron sat on the concrete step and thought about white skin and the way it looked in the moonlight. He smoked another cigarette until the halfway-mark where he could no longer hold it well. But when he was able to calm himself and return to his spot he found his moon had a banded cloud marring its face.

□ □ □

The market gave away some of its unsold goods after the work day to lepers, on the understanding that no one would show up and wait for handouts during clean hours. If they wanted to look at the food before buying it they must not touch anything, nor lean too far over the boxes full of iced fish and lobster or crates of bananas and oranges with occasional spiders dancing across them. They had to point to the items they wanted and then go and stand outside again and the grocer would put those things in paper bags and bring them outside and set them down on the ground and then when he had left again they could come forward and pick their things up.

When Claron returned home with his groceries there was a small package on his front door step. *I am not afraid to come back here and sit with you,* it said on the front cover. After putting away the food he lit a cigarette and lay down, but sleep would not come again so early and he rose and went out back with the package and tore open the cover. It was a copy of the *Book of Mormon,* and she had signed the inside cover: *They tell me you were an educated man and that you read and write not just good french and english but also spanish too. Is that right? I would love to come talk with you some time. No rush.* It was signed M.P. and then underneath the initials, as an addendum: *Maureen Pfettig.*

Claron sat with the book for a good long while. Finally he placed it down in the grass by the edge of his property and went inside to get one of the sealed cartons of milk he had just brought home. He opened the seal with his teeth and poured the milk out on the flipping pages, watching a little puddle form where the ants were already beginning to gather.

□ □ □

The next package that arrived turned out to be a book entitled *Can You Hear Me, God?* with an American ten dollar bill marking one chapter (the page had also been folded) and several colorful *gourdes* marking a citation at the end in the bibliography. *Consider this money a gift of me, Mister Claron,* the note read, *and do not think of returning it as I know you cannot make any money now days even though I hear you once had a good job here in Pétionville. And even were interested in politics? It is a wonder to me that your wife left you when you developed the troubles because you must be a fine man inside I know. M.P.*

Claron placed the second book on a small shelf alongside the first, leaving the bills in place. When the following week some flowers came wrapped in paper *(These will wilt but you know His love doesn't—I'd still like to talk to you some time whenever)* he placed them next to the books in an arrangement that was beginning to resemble a small shrine. A pamphlet describing the approaching time of the angel Moroni shining in wrath and exaltation appeared stuck alongside his door, next to the pot where once he had tried to keep a viny plant without success. *If you are ready to open your heart to me just put this brochure up on the door our signal okay?* Then came silence.

It was only after the third week of nothing that Claron realized he had stopped watching the moon, forgotten about her entirely at some point which he now in retrospect could not find. He had been reading a good deal: But what had he been reading? He stood with other beggars in town under a hot cloth and did not dwell on what could not be changed: But on what had he been dwelling? A strong windstorm hissed sand all across the beaches at night and tore pieces of his roofing away and in the morning he reset them. He went down to the water to sit in the tidepools but there had been no rain and the pools were dry, desiccated under his toes, with the colorful crabs breathing unseen bubbles now from underneath the harsh, scabbed surface. He walked into the water itself a little way, letting the rough surf wash up against him and wet to his knees. With his arms outstretched he would have pulled her light back into the sky, forced her by his will up from her hidden place over the horizon where clouds were moving like the scud that clung to his ankles. But the sky by night remained hazed in faint light, occupied and vacant at once, a teasing, distant denial. Claron was cooking his dinner again at the end of the month when she returned.

"May I come inside?" she asked. The floppy hat had been replaced by a smaller, safari-style one with a chinstrap and she was now wearing shorts and a light green shirt with a pattern on it. He could see her face clearly this time: still a young woman, a girl almost, with straight blonde hair the way white women's hair grew, and eyes that shone underneath it like small candles. The inside of one elbow had the tiny red marks of inoculation shots. She had already taken a tentative step inside his shack.

"*Non*, you may not," Claron said, and for a moment she did not respond, the small foot still touching on his floor. Then she withdrew.

"I'm not afraid to look at you," she said proudly, drawing her face up and setting her chin in the air. "I don't know how the others are around here, but I am not afraid. I know you must have had a hard life…"

"Close the door, please, and go," Claron said, having to work for a moment before he could produce the English correctly. There was a blowing disturbance in him, like the whistling sand at night, and he fought not to examine it. How he hated her, this child, this impudent! But what had he felt in her absence that he could not account for—the strange casting off, the solitude pinching at him where he had so long ago grown accustomed? Why had he left the books and the flowers she had sent, wilted dry now and brittle, in the little shrine of her gifts rather than clearing them all away? He felt a fool now for not having cleared them all away, wiped those pathetic gifts out in a storm and rush.

"I've been back in America," she asserted flatly, as if expecting him to deny this statement. "I completed my required time down here and I went back to Utah and told them all about the school we helped build, and the three churches we helped put up, two and a half really, and the petitions to the government and all the good work that's being done. Actually I was sick for a while after I came back but that passed away, you know how the water is down here. I told them about all the souls I had met, and some of the ones hopefully who were helped on their way back to Christ. I know you'll think it's presuming of me, but I told them about you."

Claron waited by the fire crackling in his stove. The bottom rim of his pot was beginning to blacken and in an automatic gesture he slid it to one side. Part of him was tempted to let the thing blister and smoke. But his pride held him.

"I told them about you and how we got to know each other, and I started to think about you. And I started to think that I hadn't yet done enough for you," she said. "Something inside me felt that way. So I went back to the council and I demanded they just find the money somewhere and let me come down here one more time. Just so I could finish with my responsibilities. That's why I came."

Claron turned himself fully toward her and for a moment her eyes dropped to the floor, the original hesitancy he had seen in her little-girl's face that first night returned and lived there. "Is it true you almost left the island when you got married?" she said, more quietly. "That your wife's father had relatives in Jamaica? But you stayed on for the school..."

He went and stood in front of her. Her eyes did not rise to look at him, staying somewhere down on the carefully-swept rugless wood. He moved closer, stood inches away from her face.

"And now the school is closed down anyway so it doesn't..."

"Why do you not look at me?" he said. *"Gade.* Look at me."

"I always said the best way to get to know people is to be pushy," she laughed suddenly, her face still averted. "Some of the loneliest people, all they want is for someone to come and *insist* on them. That's a phrase the elders teach us, to *insist* on people. And I guess you must count, because you almost died when she left you, I know that, and then when she even stopped writing. But they'll never say... nobody ever..."

"Why don't you look at me?" Claron said. "Come on, girl. Look at these hands. *Gade mem-m, wi?* Just look at my hands."

"I... I can't," she said, and he saw with some amazement that quick tears were dropping from her eyes. With absurd ease this girl-woman cried.

"Because you are afraid," he sneered. A hatred blacker than the smell of the burning dinner came and filled him suddenly. He wanted to do something to this *blan,* this child; something bad, something that would hurt her, that would *make her see.* That was it: He wanted to *force* his sight upon her.

"You are afraid, girl," he said. "Afraid!" he shouted. *"Afraid to look at this!"*

"No," she said, and now her eyes were on him with such an effortlessness of transition that Claron was silenced, the trembling rose again inside himself, the disquiet that had never left since she first came to his beach. "It's not that I don't want to see you. But when I try... when I look at you... it's like there's nothing there... I can't even see you now... even in my mind... even when I try, it's just this great big nowhere in front of me..."

She turned and hurried out but Claron followed her now onto the porch and into the stiff grasses. He had left his sandals inside and the evening stones were still warm under his feet.

"Listen to me, girl," he said, the English coming easily now, like a tide he had stepped away from only briefly that still could carry him far. "I've lived here for almost nine years. Right here in this place. That makes this my home. I read *Bon Nouvèl*. I read *Le Matin*. I listen to the radio, *wi*? But I don't hear anything. I don't see anything in the papers. I don't know anything about who is in and who is out in the government anymore. I do not write or speak out anymore. I haven't got anything you want."

She stood in the grass and wept.

"This isn't your home," Claron said. "Why don't you go back where you have a home? Go back with the *Utah* people. Go back to the people who want to see your *blan* face. Go far away from here. Go."

"I can't stop thinking about you," she said suddenly, still facing away. "I can't stop dreaming about you, Mister Claron. That was why the council wanted me to come back here. Even when I got home I couldn't stop thinking about you... like this... and I don't know if it's because you're too sad... or too good..."

Abruptly she turned and took hold of his hand, pressing it to her cheek. He felt the wetness there as he flinched terribly away.

"Please let me go," she cried.

Go, Claron hollered, like a curse, like a judgment from on high, returning somehow inside without knowing how he had returned and slamming his door without hearing the sound. *Go, go, go,* he cursed her, repeating it again and again before he realized that the girl had long since left and the sight of the sunburnt backs of her legs sending up thin geysers of sand with each running step was a memory only and the word itself continued echoing strongly in his head.

□   □   □

At the end of the year Claron received a letter. The post delivery man refused to come near the shacks themselves and left it with the grocer, who slid the envelope into the side of Claron's bag when he placed it on the ground. The postmark said *America Par Avion;* it had at some point been torn open and resealed, probably by police. He waited until after he had washed to read it.

The letter was written partially in English, partially in a halting attempt at Creole. Maureen apologized more than once for her misuse of his language but it was clear from her tone that she was proud to be able to construct even the simple sentences she had included. She told him she had settled down in a place called Pottain and had married a man named Jonas, a very pious and good man with a Biblical name *(it is not strictly biblical* she added *but it is close).* And handsome, though she imagined Mister Claron had been handsome too once! and she drew a smiling face next to the sentence. Jonas loved her and Jesus very much and thanks to both of them she was expecting a child this coming autumn. Of course the seasons didn't change down there but, since he was an educated man and knew about things, he knew what she meant. She hoped everything was well with him and she missed him and the missionary people too, even the Catholics who were on the wrong track. She wanted him to know he was always in her prayers.

Claron sat out behind his shack and began to smoke and then didn't strike the match. He suddenly wanted no light, nothing at all to obstruct her view. She would be coming soon, breaking across the already-brightening firmament like an announcement, like a trumpet, something large and inescapable as fire; not even the great distance of the sea could block her way. In the dark earth he reached out longingly for her with his blind hands. He could almost feel the nearness of her touch.

Garou

"**Look**," ***Ava said***, over by the open window frame. "That's him. That's the *loup garou*."

LeFay came to her side and leaned his hands against the brittle plaster that he knew had little other than a wooden framework inside it because the mission could afford no better, plaster that grew whitely, almost austerely hot in the long afternoon sun and trembled well into the evening; walls so uncertain he believed the very room in which he stood could collapse, like air, into thinness past measure. "I don't see him."

"There. Going up around the corner. By the palms."

But the vision was gone. LeFay looked at the three palms growing from one root, the landmark for which he always watched when returning to the mission, and the broad stretch of clay-dust road that led away toward St. Marc proper. Without knowing the landmarks one could easily drive past the entire compound, which was small and hidden from the crude road behind tangles of scrub. A chicken strutted out from behind one of the outhouses, its colors flaunted and ridiculous.

"He had his stick with him," Ava said, something unsettled in her voice. "They say he only comes out at twilight…"

"Ava. You sound like the *houngan*."

"I've heard him before," she pressed. "One night when I was staying in town with a little girl who had parasites and had to be rehydrated because the diarrhea was already chronic. The *loup garou* came walking through the streets just at twilight and banging his stick, knocking it against the walls of the houses and against fence railings, and calling something out again and again. The people all shut up their doors and put cloths over the windows as he went by. They think he has the Evil Eye."

"Does he?"

"He's retarded, Thomas. The Macoute gave him that stick when they came through here a year ago. They thought he was funny because he was so big and stupid, begging out in the street along with people who were twice his age or had real infirmities. They told him he could forget about living with such trash and become their *garou*, and they would see to it that he got plenty of food and liquor. In return he is supposed to keep people afraid."

"Afraid of him? Of a retarded boy?"

"No," Ava said, wrapping her arms up around herself in the expression LeFay had seen her use when discussing the most difficult cases in the ward. "Not afraid of him. He's just their... their *image* in this town. They think he's a joke, but Tonton Macoute isn't a joke. They're afraid *through* him."

"And?"

"And..." she began, then backed away from the window and sat once more in the wicker chair that creaked even at her small weight. It was the first thing he had noticed about her place when she finally invited him into it, absurdly long now after they had met each other and then exchanged letters when he was back in the states and then met each other again; and a long time even after that feeling had come whereby it seemed they had known each other always: the big wicker chair like something from a children's illustrated book of the Caribbean. After that he saw the copy of the Lord's Prayer that had been written out longhand, in English and in French and with the addendum in English *by this conquer,* by the old priest who had lived in this room half a century before and whose memory was so important to her, though the face in the photograph had faded almost to disappearing. He saw the map of the island with smuggling routes to the D.R. and ports marked out in red; the spiky conch shell she had found by the water and cleaned out with an alcohol solution that made the color for some reason glow absurdly vibrant; the little crucifix held up inside the dangling sheets of mosquito netting like something that had been caught there. LeFay thought he knew something about her from all these things; he collected them in his own mind and merged them to fill in the picture he had of her with all of its stern and unspoken gaps.

"And I'm afraid of him too," Ava finished. "Not of him. I'm afraid *through* him, only not like these people are afraid. My fear..."

She stopped and LeFay resettled himself on the edge of the cot where they had been sitting. He had not meant to come to St. Marc this evening. He had been quiet in his hotel room after eating a questionable dinner with a table full of Italian reporters who had almost come to blows over the question of "historical inevitability," when word had come in that there were shootings going on up north, some kind of military action that was alternately described as a push against Duvalier loyalists by other factions and extermination of other factions by Duvalier loyalists. What they had found was a small *ra-ra* in the street where one drunken man had an American-made Uzi and was firing it alternately into the air and into the dirt. The others had turned around and LeFay, having come halfway, cursed himself for several minutes before coming to see her again.

"Your fear is deeper than theirs?"

Ava smiled a little but it was the vanishing smile, and she would not look at him.

"Yes. My fear is deeper than theirs. I'm afraid for the whole country, for all these people. I'm afraid for us all."

"Ava," he said. "Come back with me. Come back to America now. This week." And she smiled but it was the same smile again, and he knew he had not reached her.

"When I saw that boy coming through the streets that night in St. Marc, I felt... I don't know if I can explain it," she said. "I sat inside the room after the father of the little girl had put cloth over the heads of the statues of Jesus so the *garou* couldn't see through them and waited for that sound to begin, the sound of him knocking the stick against the side of a house, against a rail, throwing it down into the dirt. Every time it ended I was only waiting for it to begin again. With every knock it was an ending and a beginning. I was afraid they were going to hear my heart, it was beating so loudly. And I was glad the windows were covered then because I didn't want them to see. I didn't want them to see the American, the Christian believer, the *infirmière* feeling all those things."

"But what had you to be afraid of?"

"Unless you've lived here, Thomas, you don't know what's inside that sound," she said, after a pause. "You fly in here and take pictures of these people suffering and stay for a little while in American hotels before flying out again. I lay on the floor holding that little girl's hand in mine and watching the IVAC meter click every sixty-one seconds and praying, just praying to God that the *garou* would keep on walking, that he would pass away from this house, from this side of town, that we wouldn't be marked with the sound coming closer and closer like a moving finger. When it got to the houses only three and four away from us I thought I was going to cry out loud. He came right up to the one where I was sitting and listening with that sick girl's hand in mine and then he stopped."

"He didn't strike that house?"

"He didn't strike at all. It was as if he was standing outside, just standing there and looking at the house, looking at me inside the house, and I could feel his Zinglin eyes on me. You don't know how dangerous these people are, Thomas. Nobody does. Not the Americans, not the French, no one who is trying to use them as a pawn in some other game. These people are capable of doing anything."

LeFay lay back across the cot and watched the slow turn of the ceiling fan.

"I sat there in the darkness for minutes. For minutes, just sitting there with only the breathing of that little girl and waiting to hear that other sound, waiting to hear it strike. I wanted to go over to the window and throw off the curtain and shout at him, scream something out at him, tell him to do it now and have done with it. But then I heard the next strike. I thought it would kill me to hear the next strike, I truly thought it would go through the deepest part of my heart like a knife. But when I heard it it was already at the end of the street. He had passed by the house and was moving away. Eventually I could hear some kids kicking a tin can around somewhere in the neighborhood. And that was all that happened."

"Ava," LeFay said. "I'm not going to be staying here past the end of the summer. I've already been talking to Stuart about it and they want me back in the States. It's what I want, too. I want you to think about coming with me."

This time she looked up at him and LeFay felt the small length of the room an uncrossable distance; he felt again that he was as far from her as if they had never met and he had stayed on the upper side of the Caribbean, which was like a dream world to him now but which at one time had only been home. He wanted to tell her how he would take her to a place he knew near the Chesapeake Bay where the bluefish came in by the schools and moved under your boat like a silk drape, like something untouchably fine, of an area of woods he knew in the Pioneer Valley in Massachusetts where deer ran and no one hunted them, where a house could be made in the quiet of woods full of life that is only quiet while man builds in it and then when he sleeps moves back into its life, its own sounds, and he can be in the middle of it then, he is moving in its stream. She came and sat next to him.

"Do you believe in God?" she asked.

"Ava."

"You have to tell me, Thomas. I promise I won't change the way I see you no matter what you say. But you have to tell me."

"I believe God is very important to you. I know you believe very strongly that what happens to us, what you do down here, is because God wants you to."

"Tell me, Thomas. Tell me."

He waited a moment, not looking into the sadness of her eyes. "No," he said. "Not really."

"Then can I tell you something about myself?" He was amazed to see her face and how it had not changed, how she still looked at him and into him with that inquisitiveness that was almost like a light in her expression, the kind of delicate gusted light that comes before rain.

"Yes."

"When I was a little girl I lived in Iowa. My grandparents had a farm there—what was left of a farm. It didn't produce anymore, not since my grandfather's days, but they still owned the land. There were no neighbors around us for miles, and I had no sister and no brother. Instead I would go walking, walking as far as I could reach in a day, as soon as school was out or as soon as church was out or as soon as my father would let me go from the house, I would walk for hours. And the places I went became my places. They were nothing, a grove of trees or a dirty stream hidden in some woods... but they were *my* places. Not because anyone had given them to me—not because they were a gift, or because they were my inheritance, or because there was any reason in the world for me to have them. But I *saw* them, Thomas, I got there on my own power and I *saw* them and I *knew* them. And every place I went, every day farther than I had been, that place became one of my places. I kept it with me. Do you understand that?"

"All right."

"But do you understand?"

LeFay thought about it. She went on:

"One day I found a robin's nest in the crook of a barn roof. It was made out of yellow grass and sticks and the bowl had been woven together as if by hands, it was carefully pieced together from nothing at all until it had substance, until it was strong and a place for life. I was amazed at the twisting together of stems, of twigs, amazed at the way it was built, the way it *made sense*. There were eggs in it, three large ones and a small, speckled with color. We didn't use that barn for anything then, it had been sagging for years in a far corner of the property, all weeds and scraggle and rained-out planks of wood falling in. I don't think anyone really remembered it was there. Every day I went back to that place up in the loft, I leaned out over the edge of the loft to see those eggs. On the third day the eggs were cracked open, and there were chicks in the nest, their heads wet and new and uncertain, and they were nothing but those open beaks, the open hungry beaks. I thought they were the weakest things in the world.

"I came back the next day with earthworms I dug up from my

mother's garden and cut into pieces. And I leaned over from the railing and fed them to the chicks, one piece at a time, handing them into the nest and into the little mouths. I was leaning over and holding on with one arm and I could feel the air from the barn filling up inside my clothes, the hay smell and the seed smell moving over me. And the next day when I came back the mother robin had knocked all her chicks out of the nest."

"Because you touched them."

"That's right. Because I touched them."

She came to his side now and sat next to him and LeFay put his arm around her back, feeling the too-visible bones and the tightness there, and wishing for the loosening feeling he knew a woman gives when she wants her shoulders to be covered by a man's arm, wishing for it and not feeling it.

"That was when I first thought that I understood Christ," she said. "What he wanted to do with his life, what he had tried to become. I don't know if I can explain it any better than that."

There was a pause, liquid, untense.

"I should go," LeFay said after a while, beginning to disengage himself. "Stuart asked me to phone..."

"Thomas," she said.

□　□　□

At five in the morning LeFay awoke under the ceiling fan. It had ceased turning when the mission shut down its electricity at midnight and hung now like a symbol of something, linking up to his vague thoughts as they dissipated into the air. Ava was there, her back turned against him, bare skin showing down to the level of the sheeting. He looked at that skin and then back at the ceiling and he thought about things, and came to certain decisions and forgot them and resolved those same issues once more, letting the nighttime move behind his eyes. When he opened them again the face of the dead priest was just visible hovering from the far wall, his expression vague in the slim first hint of light that was not yet light. And the second time he heard it he knew why he had awakened, knew, even as he cursed it, that he had been expecting it all night, even from his sleep and the place where dreams would go but none emerge.

Ava, he thought. You are the last thing there will ever be. There is you and then if there is not you, there is a great empty space large enough to swallow up the stars.

Ava, he thought. When I was twenty-five I went to Phnom Penh for the first time, trying to get as far away from everything I knew as possible. I saw a woman there punished by soldiers by having chopsticks driven up her nose. When I was twenty-seven I was living in Belfast. I was a stringer for the Associated Press, full of the world. At twenty-nine I was in Israel. I was a stringer. At thirty I was back in Phnom Penh, where I and one other man who was older but knew almost nothing about the business started the photography bureau for the *Agence France Presse,* because they did not know how young I was by wire. Then Morocco, then Belfast again. In Belfast I woke up crying once almost ten years after the fact because of the woman with the chopsticks.

Ava, he thought. I have to go home now.

He looked out toward the window where the sound was coming. Somewhere in the moon-dusted street the *garou* was swinging his stick, knocking the end against the dull flat soundlessness of tree boles and the sudden sharp ring of metal walls. The knocking was regular, almost rhythmic, the audible step of something that walked in the predawn colors with feet that carried themselves through the air like the tread of a clock. LeFay listened to the knocking move through the houses and when he had convinced himself that it was not coming closer, he put his arm around the woman lying next to him and drew her near. She was tense against his skin like something in a vise, something resisting, and he stayed next to her, breathing her breathing and waited for her muscles to relax. In a moment and though she had not changed, he became aware that she was awake.

"It's him, isn't it?" Ava said, unmoving.

"Yes," LeFay said. "Yes it is."

"Is he coming this way?"

"No," LeFay said. "Not tonight."

After a minute she slept again and LeFay lay peering at the dim not-light that was building in the little room, the half-seen, half-unseen that was the world trickling and inching along the floor and through the moted air. The face of the old man on the wall seemed to be watching him.

The Talking

The body was slumped up a little way into the grove of low-hanging banyan and creepers, off behind the cemetery wall where there were rows and rows of bullet-punches left in the brick. Every day when Joseph Lord Maitre passed this place he swung over by the wall and let his fingers drag in and out of the scratchy punch-marks. These, he knew, were left from times the Macoute stood people up against the cemetery's edge, looking in over the wall at the graves, and made them choose which side of the yard they would like to lie in. It was a game the Macoute played with people, who a few minutes before had been walking down Rue Alerte with their hands full of sweet yellow mangoes they were going to eat for lunch or bright nails to build something, and certainly not thinking about which side of the graveyard they would want to lie in or how the dirt would taste in their mouths when they fell down. That was the part Joseph always added in: how the dirt tasted when it filled up your whole face and eyes.

Of course, Joseph knew, it didn't matter which side you chose. Most of the time they took you away somewhere and there was never any burial at all, except the empty caskets he sometimes saw being carried across town as if it were a real funeral, the family stopping and tipping the top wide over an undug grave to show there was nothing inside, at which point the women would begin to wail and the men would look at their feet and rearrange things in their pockets. Joseph did not know where the bodies really went, although he was aware the Macoute took them away somewhere rather than let them talk, which is what his friend Bien Salut told him would happen. If you left a dead man lying right there in the street the way they used to, sometimes someone would pull on the dead man's arm and call into his ear: "Who done this thing to you, Paul Marzan? Who done this, Luc Jolio?" And the body would answer from inside its unmoving mouth: "Damon LaFice, who owed me money and is now a Macoute." When Bien Salut explained this part, he imitated the dead man speaking with his lips stretched wide and moving them as little as possible, signifying the passage of unearthly breath. "Damon LaFice, Petre Aubon, Jon Salain..." And the townspeople would gather stones and metal bars and go destroy the houses of whomever the body had said, breaking down everything, even pulling out the toilet. Bien had been clear on this last part.

But this one must have been forgotten by the Macoute, or perhaps they had dragged him back into the shady place where Joseph's eye just happened to go, expecting no one would see it. If he hadn't been swinging the satchel and running at the same time, with his head down low and the hot sun flashing bright in his eyes as he went, he thought he might not have seen it either. He put down the satchel with his books—*English Reader One, Hygiene, A Taste of Salt*—and stepped carefully through the high grasses and overgrowth until he was next to the dead man's feet.

The dead man was sitting with his back against the graveyard wall where it was lowest, and his legs were a little bent with his arms down at his sides. His shirt was open and Joseph could see the skin on his narrow, hairless chest and the little St. Christophe medallion that he wore. The dead man's expression was one of concern; eyes closed tightly but as if only for the moment, his mouth tight too as if he were concentrating. Bottle-green flies and mosquitoes passed around him, and Joseph wondered now if a mosquito would bite a dead man because his blood was no longer alive. He watched carefully until he saw one land on the unmoving cheek but he could not tell if it bit.

□   □   □

His mother's name was Francine Maitre but where she worked she had another name: *La Feu*. Joseph threw his satchel onto the steps of the pink-and-blue building where some men were sitting around out front and drinking out of paper cups, but none of them paid him any mind. His face was as regular here as his mother's, and often she sat with him on the front steps and rocked him against her leg while the sun was setting gigantic over the hills of Pétionville, and when he got too big for her leg he would sit at her side and say *allo* to the men as they came up the steps. It was the English word they had learned first in school. The men always said *allo* to him and every so often one of them would say *allo* to Francine as well, in a smiling, smiling kind of way, and then Francine would be *La Feu* and she would have to get up and go inside the pink-and-blue building with the man for a while. When she came out and found him again she always smelled different.

Joseph knew what his mother was doing inside the building: she was fucking the men. He knew this because Bien Salut had told him that was what men did at the pink-and-blue house, and then he had swiveled his hips around in a grinning circle and demonstrated something with his fingers. It took Joseph a little while to understand the relevance of the finger motion but in time he got it: that was fucking, and it was what his mother did with men, except that when they drank too much out of their

paper cups while waiting for the women to show up in the evenings, sometimes they could not get their fuckers back up.

"Jesus does not want to hear such talk," the teacher at the
mission school said when he asked her why the men drank so
much they couldn't get their fuckers up. She was a *Baptist* from
Lou-siana who got the Jesus for the third world, and she always
stood with two fingers tight on the chalk and her pin-eyes quiver-
ing while she waited for someone to answer her question in
English. She made him go into the bathroom where there was a
picture of God over the mirror and wash his mouth out with soap
for saying such a thing. Joseph refused to do it and she told him
from the other side of the door he had better do it like a sorry
boy or as Jesus knew she would not let him out, and he stood in
the dark and cold tiled bathroom for a long time before the door
burst suddenly open and the woman grabbed him with one arm
and forced the soap rhythmically into his mouth three times
before he was able to run out, spitting little pieces from behind
his teeth. "I'll scrub that dirty mouth of yours white," she said.

Now he sat on the steps of the pink-and-blue building and
watched the sun breaking up the line of palm trees and heavier,
broken trees up near the hills while he waited for Francine to
show. He found that if he squinted directly into the rim of the sun
after a few minutes the hills all seemed to blend, a great flaming
confusion. It was not the only pink-and-blue building in
Pétionville, in fact most houses were pink or blue or no-color; but
the pink-and-blue building was easily spotted because it was pink
on one side and then a blue part ran up one third of the front,
breaking from the rest in a clean line, as if the painters had run
out of one color before they could finish the job. In the daytime
Francine worked as a maid at the Baptist Clergy House on the
other side of town; Joseph had not seen that building, but he
imagined it was the color of deep red earth.

"How you today, boy," one of the men who were drinking on the steps called over to him. The man was oldish and had white powder in his hair and even in his eyebrows, and his eyes were always dirty in the white parts and jelly-like. He certainly drank a lot, and Joseph wondered sometimes how he could get his fuckers up when he needed to. But Joseph didn't mind him speaking. The men were always nice.

"I saw a body by the school," Joseph said, turning with his hands on the cinderblock stoop. "Saw a dead guy."

The older man grunted assent; he understood about such things. Another said something about the heat, and two who had been knocking a handful of dominos around nodded voicelessly. It was very hot in the hour just before the shadows broke free like rain and evening came. In a little while a woman who worked with his mother but was not his mother came by, jogging hurriedly up the steps in a colorful dress and hoop earrings. The men became very happy when they saw her; the ones who had been slow-moving and like sleeping men spoke to her with enthusiastic new voices. She told them they would have to wait just a few minutes more and then she would be ready for one or two of them, the *tap-tap* had gotten stuck in mud but she would call out the upper window when she was ready. She had some packages in one hand. On the way past Joseph she stopped and ran her fingers archly across his hair.

"How is my Bien today?" she asked.

"He's okay," Joseph said. "He went right home after school."

□   □   □

A group of branches dipped down around the graveyard like covering arms, and just for a moment Joseph thought that the body had moved. From where he was walking, looking and pretending not to look with one hand running over the scratchy pock-marked wall, he could not see it, and it occurred to him that perhaps it was only the wind making the dry leaves gyrate and the light fall down just so that had let him see where the dead man was sitting. Then he dropped his satchel and jumped into the creepers and spear grass, swatting his hands at the tiny black flies and gnats that swarmed up from their disturbed wells and onto his legs. The dead man was still there.

"How you today, boy?" Joseph asked.

The dead man seemed to consider the question, his graying face working hard against an appropriate response.

"How you?" Joseph said loudly. "Me, sure, I'm okay. Sure I am okay."

Joseph pushed a little way more into the heated gloom. On closer examination he found the place on the man's belly where he had been shot; it was why the shirt was hanging a little bit open and the medallion visible. Two of the plastic buttons had been broken apart by the bullets so it was open in the middle and closed again at the top. Joseph looked at the holes and for a moment almost touched one, thinking that they did not look large enough holes to have hurt him very badly. But there he was, dead man, dragged back into the grass and trees and talking to no one. The pockets of his jeans were all turned inside out. Between his unmoving fingers some faster blades had already started growing.

Joseph sat next to the dead man and tried to think what would be the appropriate thing to say. He did not want to touch the dead man's arm or lean too close to his ear. The dead man's fingers had gone gray around the edges like his face and he seemed to be holding only tentatively to the earth, seeking assurance from what he could feel but no longer see.

"What's it like, in there?" Joseph tried, quiet. "Is it bad?"

The dead man was silent, considering.

"I guess it's not so bad," Joseph said. "I guess if it was so bad, you'd say something about it. So I guess it's not so bad at all. I bet it doesn't even hurt so much."

The dead man seemed to assent. Joseph saw that something wet had congealed around his eyelids, sticking them together like wax.

"Well, I got to get home now," Joseph said, after a while. "You be good."

□ □ □

Bien Salut assured him it would work: you had to pull on the right arm and shout into the left ear, and you had to shout hard because the dead are so far away, it's like calling into a sewer pipe. Further, if they were to go to the *bokor* and purchase a package of salt wrapped carefully in paper and put it in the mouth of the dead man, the body would rise at night and do whatever they told it to. It could see the future or carry them on a trip through the sky, although if the package ever broke somehow and the zombi tasted the salt, it would turn and throw them down from a cliff and then tear the *bokor* himself to pieces, like the people with bricks and iron bars tore apart the houses of the Macoute, including the toilets. But Bien wanted to know why he had all these questions about zombis.

"*De rien,*" Joseph said.

Joseph lived with his three sisters and the grandmother in a little house beside the *Katolik* church, but since it was *Katolik* and it was the Baptists who had given Francine the job as a maid neither he nor his sisters nor grandmother set foot in the church at all. His grandmother said it would have been very bad *djok* to be servant to both the spirits Baptist and the spirits *Katolik,* the spirits would war and tear at each other like dogs. And Francine agreed; it could only lead to trouble. Perhaps she would lose her job, or the grandmother might have another bout of the fever. Joseph hated thinking of that, because the last time the grandmother had the fever she started seeing *loa* talking to her, and now when she needed the bathroom she didn't always make it out of the house.

Francine always kept her eyes straight when passing the *Katolik* church, her hands on the knot in front of her dress and her chin a little bit high. Every few months the mission people came by their house looking for people to change Gods, but Francine sent them away. One morning a white priest had been standing on the steps where a little statue of the Virgin was and called down to her, "The angels are happier for one come back than ten who never strayed, *ma seu.*"

"*Damballa,* defend," Francine answered, not turning.

Joseph was at home standing in the street when the woman came by. She was wearing a strange printed shirt with a silver cross visible around her throat where the skin hung down in a little flap and had her hair tied back tight under her hat as if she were afraid someone might touch it. She had on heavy gardening gloves to block the sun and was holding a bag in front of her like it was protecting her from something, and she stood in the street just outside the little fence made of cactus and wire where their house was, not coming inside.

"Look at the crazy *blan,*" his sister said, catching the plastic hoop they were throwing as it came down and holding onto it for a minute. She had been throwing it hard, trying to hurt Joseph with the broken rim where a sharp edge stuck out, but now she forgot her malice. Joseph went to the edge of the cactus. His teacher's water-colored eyes quivered.

"You are not to come to *l'école* any more, Joseph Lord Maitre," she said. "Tell your mother that we know all about the way she... about how she makes her living. And we cannot have that in our mission." His teacher seemed to hesitate, lips tight. The she walked away, stopping to look over at the *Katolik* church grimly as if she saw something there she had expected all along.

That night when Francine came home Joseph did not say anything, hearing her move as quietly as she could about the house with her strange smells from fucking with the different men. She took off her clothes and just as she was lying down next to the grandmother Joseph's sister said, "A crazy *blan* came by to see Joseph."

"Papa Legba," the grandmother began. *"Oh, Papa Legba.* Not more trouble."

"What did she want, Joseph?" his mother sighed. He could hear the thinness in her voice.

"De rien," he said.

□   □   □

Joseph sat on the bare floor next to the mattress where his mother was fucking. After a while the man, who was heavy and had patchy-looking skin, made a funny grunting noise and then lay still, and Joseph thought he was asleep. He watched the electric fan turning its slow loops and after a while Francine reached a hand down toward him and he held her fingers, which she painted bright red on the nails whenever she became *La Feu*. "You go on and run now," she whispered when she was able to get her head over to his side of the mattress. "I won't be but another hour."

So he walked down the rickety steps and out the front of the building where it was cool night and shadows, and fewer men waiting. They had all been very happy when Francine showed up tonight, and Joseph thought there must have been some kind of *politicaille* nearby. The men were always more happy and drank more and sat on the steps more after *politicaille*, which could happen in front of the bishop's house or in front of a tax collector's house or anywhere there was room for people to gather. At the Baptist school they told him *ra-ras* were from Satan, like not washing your hands before you eat. Bien Salut told him that rallies happened when *the people's mind is one,* and for a while Joseph had tried to picture how that came about: people standing around in the market, knocking lobsters against wood blocks and tying up the claws, or haggling over rice and coffee the way his sister did. The people look at one another, first slightly and then more and more; a *ra-ra* begins. But he was unsure.

"Hey now boy," the old man with the salty-white brows roared when he saw Joseph coming fast down the steps. His face was almost closed over with the drink and the breath grumbled on down in his lungs long after he had finished speaking. "How's all your things?"

"It's okay," Joseph said. Someone was lighting a bottle rocket in the street and Joseph watched the tail end burn and not ignite. He jumped sideways off the porch and out onto the sidewalk.

"You be good," the old man called after him.

□   □   □

There was no doubt about it now; the body was moving. He had been here three times since his *blan* teacher came and told him not to come to their *blan* school any more, each time taking his satchel with him in the mornings after his bath the way he always did, and leaving his satchel in the ivy and tall grass where he sat instead with the dead man.

The first time the dead man started speaking it had not really surprised him. He realized only later that he had, in fact, been talking for some time, like a colorful lizard clicking and clicking in the grass, before Joseph thought to notice it. The dead man would speak but he would not listen, he did not seem to understand Joseph was on the other side of his body and sometimes saying things to him, trying to answer back, and so after a while Joseph gave up. The dead man talked on, not seeming to notice.

But his body had changed. The hard grass was now not only growing up from between his fingers where they lay but it had poked up inside his hands and come out the backs of them, raising the shirt sleeve a little bit where it stood as it grew all the way up inside his arm. The expression on the dead man's face showed consternation, Joseph thought, over this; he seemed not worried but given pause; and that was not all. There were thick creeper vines coming around and up through the holes in his stomach where the bullets had gone through, new yellow just-forming leaves showing their heads. Joseph sat next to the dead man in the mottled light, leaning himself up against the wall.

"You best not talk that way," he said, "I'm gon' have to wash that dirty mouth away white. You watch out now."

The dead man chattered on, speaking quietly. His voice sounded lonely, an expression of some far-away sorrow, like the voice of someone standing at the shore during a wind and speaking out into the air when it swallows up all the sound.

"You watch it," Joseph said. "Just watch out."

□　□　□

On Friday morning Francine saw him in town. He had just been walking around, meaning to find something that he felt vaguely he had set down somewhere in the hot streets where the sellers were calling out and the charcoal-men were digging deep pits to burn in and the smell of cooking pig and fried chicken was around and on him, as if under his skin. He saw Francine coming toward him from a part in the crowd.

"Why ain't you in that school?" she cried, amazed. Her hair had rubber bands and ribbons in it and she was wearing her *La Feu* dress with the plastic red bracelets. A man stood to one side of her, holding onto the small part of her dress from the back.

"Ain't no more school," Joseph said. She hit him across the face.

"What you mean, ain't no more school? What that mean?" Francine said, eyes huge. Joseph started to cry.

"What you mean, ain't no more school?" Francine shouted.

"That school got tore to pieces," Joseph hollered out, frantic. "You ask Simone. Bad people came and tore that school up to pieces and all us had to go home."

Francine looked at him bawling with her amazed expression unchanged. The man standing behind her gradually widened his mouth into a smile, revealing bright silver teeth.

□   □   □

"*Legba, oh, Papa Legba,*" the grandmother moaned. The sisters were crying, and Joseph, although he was crying as well, did not feel himself to be. After several hours he felt himself only empty, a socket in the air that stood where once he had been.

"It's all right," Francine was saying to his grandmother. "It's all right, I'll still get money. You know I'll still get money somewhere."

His grandmother said that it was the house next to a *Katolìk* church, she had known all along since they moved into it that the deal was unwise. The Baptist spirits had found out where they were living; they could sense it on her when she came in to work at the Clergy House. Everyone knew that *Katolìks* were *kominis,* and worse; some said that they drank the blood of dying men, or each other's blood. The signs had been very bad, although the house was large and had cool crushed-shell walls, she had known, she had known.

"It's all right, *manman,*" Francine said, stroking the old woman's scalp that to Joseph was like the hide of an alligator or a paper bag, a grocery bag woman, hair and skin that had started to fade with her great age.

"Papa Legba, Legba," the grandmother crooned.

"It be all right, *manman,*" Joseph said to his mother, but her eyes flashed and he knew not to speak. He had lied to her, had shamed her by making her go into work at the Clergy House for a week when no one there was able to tell her why the *blan* ministers all looked away and coughed into their hands when she came in, why they seemed to want to tell her something but everyone was waiting for someone else to tell it. Then the end of the month came and the little man who paid her would not give her any money. Then she had understood.

Joseph went outside to the front of the house and listened to his sisters crying inside and looked at the stars over town. There was a *ra-ra* in town tonight and Bien Salut had told him that people were going to die at it, that it was an inevitable river the people were running. He heard sounds from beyond the closest houses but could not tell if they were fireworks or guns. After a while Francine came out and stood next to him.

"Papa Legba," she sighed, putting her arm around Joseph's shoulders. Her anger seemed to have slipped from her like a passing breeze. She did not even seem aware that she touched him. "Now I have to be up in that house every day."

The white priest came and stood out on the front steps of the *Katolik* church and lit some candles and stood looking also at the sky. Francine looked at him and then seemed to think about it for a little while and when the priest was finished she took her arm off Joseph and started toward the church.

For the first few steps Joseph followed her down the street, walking the way they always walked mornings only now the road was hidden and night crackled and hissed around them; after a while he was walking by himself and then he was running, hurrying past the town center where men were gathering in a little crowd and shouting *Boule kay! Boule kay!* at another man who was standing up on a series of crates with a burning stick in one hand, spilling flutter-light over all their faces. He hurried on past the near-empty streets where men and women leaned up against the walls and smoked and drank tafia, until he was at the cemetery.

In the utter gloom beneath the limbs of trees he at first could not find the body. A sudden voice in him said it had risen completely and walked away with the coming of night, a packet of salt wrapped carefully in cloth weighting down its tongue; it was walking even now through the stars. Then he found it, chattering and talking away all by itself in their secret place where it sat, only now it had slumped over a bit and was not sitting comfortably. Green thick branches and the heavy flowers of weeds rose up through the torso and the sagging back, and every second inch of the body was grass. The mouth chattered and spoke, chattered and spoke, and from under the lid of one gripped-shut eye came a thin clean blade of plant. Joseph was aware now that they were all like that: all the bodies in the graveyard that had chosen where they wanted to lie, all the bodies of the men in the fucking house, all the Baptists and *Katoliks*. All of them spoke, all of them talking and talking and together making one voice that was coming at him like a tide, like this body where he sat with the dung beetles clicking and chattering now up and out of its working mouth. The talk would scrub him white. It would make him clean.

Away Down South

At first things looked quite bad, LeFay thought: the inspections men were wearing blue along with the innocuous gray and tan uniforms. Blue shirts with zippers up the front rather than buttons, blue pants underneath the standard top. He wasn't certain how to read it. Then the customs man who checked their bags was wearing mirrored shades and he knew things were bad, things were very bad. But the inspection went by without any comment and they were sent along to the waiting terminal while the grimy old-generation airplanes from Air Haïti and the better-dressed ones from United and TWA nosed the asphalt outside with their front tires and things looked considerably better.

"Isn't the airport government-run?" LeFay asked when he believed there was no one close enough to hear them. It was still possible that somebody was going to come by before the plane taxied up, even after it had taxied up, even after they were seated on it and the door was closed and the engines were gunning. Really you were not safe until you were in the air and Port-au-Prince was a gray and red diamond receding underneath you into that incredible expanse of Caribbean blue, blue so untamed it justified in his mind the usage of French terminology: *azure*. "What are Macoute doing in here?"

"There's not as much difference between them as there once was," Ava said. She had her bag slung up around one shoulder and did not rest it on the carpet, in the manner of travelers untrustful of their environment and used to having to leave quickly. "I'm not sure if there ever was a difference, really. Cagoulard, Macoute, the military junta. One can become the other rather easily." She scanned the waiting room in the same manner as LeFay, both their expressions kept slack and revealing no emotion: only in hers, LeFay thought, there was something other than the studied nonchalance of the foreigner on foreign soil. He didn't want her to know it was there.

"Maybe someone is bringing the groups together for a push. Maybe this is Namphy's strategy. Hell, maybe it's Baby Doc's own strategy." He watched her face.

"More likely it's the U.S.," she said, and LeFay heard the missionary in her voice. "They have every interest in keeping this country at its own throat. They aren't going to let unification happen down here, even among the insurgents. Bring together the gangs to destabilize the people at the top, who were set in place by Tonton Sam to begin with. Then set the gangs fighting again. It's so common it's almost stated policy."

"Now you sound like an agitator," LeFay said, but he was unable to raise a smile. Then looking at her he saw it was coming and he turned aside instead and watched the Air Haïti planes out front with their odd single-digit wheels, and the sun standing out fantastically on groups of ragged trees with wide green hair. If only it wouldn't come for another twenty minutes they would be away from here, they would be in one of those grimy and unsafe-looking planes and then things could be different, really different. But it was here now and he knew it as he heard her bag settle to the rug and still he didn't want to turn and face her.

"Thomas," she said. "I can't do this. It was wrong for me to say I could."

"Too late to make a stand for Christ now," he answered, still not looking at her. "Stuart's already spotted our tickets. They'd be crestfallen if I came to the office dinner party with no date." But he was speaking too easily about it, and something in him shifted.

"Thomas," she said, and he felt her warm, strong small hands on his back and the side of her face leaning against his back. In his mind he could see her so clearly it was amazing to him, because he did not turn around; could see the expression on her face, the lonely but determined-to-be-lonely expression there that was the kind Jesus most prized, that was just the attitude desired by a God who loved his creatures so much he chose never to speak to them again after one three-year stint in a desert.

"Ava, in America..." he began, but it was useless. Still he heard himself saying: "In America... back home in America..."

"No," she said, holding him from behind a little and the side of her face pressing against his shirt so he could feel her. "I can't run away from all this. You know that I can't. You can come back and see me whenever you want. But there isn't anything for me in..."

"There isn't anything *here*," LeFay said strongly, and now he did turn around and her face was almost as he had known it would be. "Think about this. It isn't just that there isn't anything for you here. It isn't just that, although God knows that's enough."

"Thomas, don't speak like..."

"It isn't just that. Although that should be enough. It's that there isn't anything *here* at all. There isn't anything *on this island* at all. Don't you understand that yet? You're standing here in the middle of the ocean on a spot that only exists just enough for you and people like you to stand on it, and other than that it isn't even out here. It probably exists under your feet as you walk only enough to keep you from falling, because you choose for it to be here. But that's all."

"Then that's enough," she said, not melodramatically; and there was not that thing in her face that he knew would not be there, that thing of needing that he felt in his own face and knew was in himself. She was tired, yes; she had a fatigue he would probably never know. But the fatigue did not bring into her the needing thing, the hollow; that was his own. "That's enough for me," she said. "That's all it has to be. If I can make the island better by choosing to stand..."

"There is no island," LeFay said, and again he turned away so the needing thing and the hollow thing would not show in him, and he knew it, so that it was not necessary to hide this from himself. "All these missionary people, Ava, they're all standing in the water. It's the best trick Jesus has pulled in two millennia. And all they ever have to do is look down to see there is only waves under their feet."

"Poor Thomas," she said. "Is that really what has happened to you? But I saw that the first day you came here. I saw that the very first day."

Then she was gone. There had been more between them, more saying of things and some touching, but it had grown quickly to a gray undifferentiated area that sounded too much like other gray undifferentiated areas he had in his memory. It had faded at that point and only the living words stayed still with him, that much of a living conversation. She had kissed him also but all that was gray.

He sat in the plane that had taxied into place after crossing the striped asphalt, and no one had stopped him at the last gate, nor at the little fold-down steps that descended from the door, nor on the plane itself. Now he sat by the inner window with his baggage stowed away somewhere above him and enough French and Italians working their way around that it was safe to be just a journalist again, there was no threat now. He heard the three- and four-language banter going back and forth between the close-built seats and even in the languages he could not follow it sounded like home. He told himself he would not sit and stare out the window for her, certainly not look for her, nor look at the island itself which was already fading in sunlight like a badly-done print, like an antique photo that is going to the bland. But he looked and she was not there nor anywhere. A young man crouched outside by the base of the trees.

LeFay looked at him instead, rather than the dissolving land that soon would be a patina and hardly even a memory: the young man, more than a boy but young still, with narrow, strong features in his body visible even underneath the formal jacket and pants that stood out because they were not official airport clothing. He did not seem to be a workman although the others just passed him by without comment, and he was crouched and sitting by the base of a growth of palms as if waiting for something, one hand up lightly underneath his chin and his face rested somehow sadly and leaning away. He had white chalk painted up across his face, all over the face, so that his skin made a background for the startling image of bones that rested there. He had no eyes.

Then the airplane moved and LeFay felt something open inside him as he leaned back in his seat, he did not think of her and instead watched the something disappearing from inside himself like the colors of water that evolved underneath the plane, the whitecaps appearing at this height in thin, penciled lines and then the reefs visible in bright green. A businessman came down the center aisle.

"See the *ra-ra?*" he laughed at LeFay, working himself into a less-cramped seat after slamming his briefcase into the overhead so hard the plastic door popped. "Just happened into the middle of it. People out in the street, dancing and drumming. Costumes all around, and in the middle of it these banners of Aristide, banners of Jesus, and a blind fellow dressed up as Baron what's-his-name. They were carrying him along on their shoulders."

The man waited but when LeFay did not respond he settled himself in a little bit more instead. "Dear God," he laughed, as if corroborating his own observation.

"*Samedi,*" LeFay said. "It means Saturday."

"You what?"

"Saturday," LeFay said. "The day in between Good Friday and Holy Sunday. The nothing day."

"Dear God," the man smiled to himself, cracking a newspaper wide like he was breaking its back.

Laborers in the Valley of the Lord:
August, 1985

They were both priests of God. The two sat together, though separated by enough of the unsmooth wood and woven mats to make the smaller man uneasy. Having had experience with confessions—the open-air kind that came after Vatican II when the forced consolation of a hard box was removed and confessor and confessant had to face each other like what they were, two mortals—he knew how to read the types of distances the confessor chose from what he perceived to be the source of benefaction and forgiveness. But perhaps the other priest did not feel him to be a source of benefaction; perhaps forgiveness was out of the question. Perhaps he—the older priest whose name, Maretin, had been changed to the English form *Martin* when his family emigrated during the occupation—was simply working through some pattern by coming to the younger man and asking to be given the sacrament, asking to be taken into his smaller room and sat at his orange-crate-turned table where he wrote letters to his sister in Cape Canaveral and listen to him, Fr. Maretin, speak, and then speak the appropriate words in response to him and pray for his forgiveness, as Maretin had asked, the way one would ask a friend to water the plants or be certain to lock a door upon exiting a room.

Fr. Maretin was well his senior. Not only in years: He was that, physically older by a decade at least, though he kept his age not so much a secret as an unknown on the compound. But his jet hair had more than a powdering of age in it, and his stern, restless face, sagged here and again against the bone. The eyes alone seemed distracted, stark blue, again with the fierceness and otherworldly quality the young priest had noticed right away. Fr. Maretin had a way of looking at nothing, as if unseen presences were scampering into the corners of rooms where he watched, unstated things that might come into actual being if he ever were to catch sight of them full on; or perhaps if he ever were to lose them.

The first time he had seen him, Fr. Maretin had been at the docks at Point Neuf. He, Fr. Kierney, had come down the Floridian straits and across the relatively brief jaunt to the island in a ship carrying several other people and medical supplies and books. He had read a copy of *The Comedians* on route as the only way he could think of to prepare himself for the unexpected assignment since the intensive French refresher and basic Creole course had ended and he had only to wait for the head of the mission to find him. The book was dull but the image of the weeping Haitian traveling in a small boat not unlike the one in which he found himself had impressed him, lingered on in his consciousness after the remainder of the story had passed away. And Fr. Maretin was there at the docks, looking not like an older priest at all in a shoulder-strap tee-shirt that showed his arm muscles, still formidable in age, not so much burnt as marauded by the sun, the only defining mark on him a thin chain of bright gold links around his sweating neck with a small crucifix attached. Fr. Kierney, sweating mercilessly in his long pants and formal jacket, had introduced himself with an air of the schoolboy imposing for a moment upon the principal.

It later turned out that Fr. Maretin had not been there at Point Neuf to meet him at all—no one had even remembered his arrival—but had been assisting with the unloading of supplies, many of which were bound for the mission and were subject to both search and seizure by the military and simple looting by the locals if someone forceful were not there to prevent it. Even that did not always help, but Fr. Maretin made a signal difference.

That was when Fr. Kierney had first noticed his eyes: cold, almost frightening blue rings with that distracted but intense motion. Not the distraction of the absent-minded but of the painter, the one who sees more than you can possibly see though you and he are gazing at the same field of wheat and the same crows; who has vision and with it the critical price of vision which, if it is not a more dangerous, more precarious hold on sanity, is at least something uncomfortably close to that.

"Forgive me, young father," the older man said, his considerable frame wrapped now in the black evening vestments and his head angled down so that he appeared to be reading from the small table on which no objects sat other than his broad, oak-like hands. "For I..."

There was a long space of silence in which Fr. Kierney began to wonder if the man was going to continue. A tropical evening had come into the room with its vague gauzy colors, and the wine cruets kept on a wicker tray in Fr. Kierney's room shone purple and blue. As Fr. Kierney watched the older priest stood, slowly, heavily, like a man carrying something. Still not meeting Fr. Kierney's embarrassed gaze and his face abruptly revealing no awareness of the younger man at all, he stepped over to the wooden cabinet on top of which the sacrificial wine sat catching the light, unstoppered the bottle, and tipped it back into his mouth.

"Father! Sir!" the younger priest cried out, jumping abruptly from his chair. He was narrow-bodied and narrow-faced and his

weak, almost reddish hair, bleached into ridiculous brightness by
this sudden exposure to the sun, gave a foolish atmosphere to his
outburst. He raised one hand as if he wanted to reject what he
was witnessing, reject it wholly. The older priest restoppered the
bottle and sat again, his eyes intense and quite absent.

"It's the Macoute," he said.

Fr. Kierney was still standing, amazed in a winded, breathy
way inside himself and yet somehow knowing that it was he himself who had been vain. He felt the accusation winging in the
room and settling about him. He sat, hands in lap.

"It's the Ma..."

"What about the Macoute?" Fr. Kierney cut him off. He
wanted there to be anger in his voice but there was not anger
there, only disrespect for the elder man, and that was not what he
had intended. The sound of his own voice hurt him. "What about
them?"

"His flowers..." Fr. Maretin began, and lapsed into a contem-
plation so grave he appeared to have forgotten once more the
other man's presence in the room; forgotten it or dismissed it as
not worth consideration.

"In the chapel?" Fr. Kierney said. "They were torn down by
street kids. Only by kids. I thought we all agreed that was not a
political statement."

Now the eyes met him and they were bear's eyes, red in their
centers where there was no color at all, and certainly not the
color red: yet the younger man felt that smolder somewhere in
them, felt more strongly than even the bright, surprising disks of
blue he actually saw. He could almost feel the pulsing blood of
capillaries there, swimming in those living eyes.

"It's an act of *Lucifer,*" the old priest hissed, his jaw bristling.
"To desecrate the holy space. To strew those flowers across the

room, across the seats and along the floor. Lucifer's followers did it. He is strong in this land."

"I don't accept..."

"He is *strong.*"

Fr. Kierney returned the stare until he could no longer, and then he rose and went to his window. Outside he could see the white-dirt pathways snaking through the compound like a badly-made map, the outdoor showers gone to rust in this salt-rich air, their pipes fronting on the infirmary building with its bright clean walls. At the end of the lane three Haitian children were playing with something dead, prodding the little carcass up with sticks and pretending to make it dance.

"I don't have anything to say about that," Fr. Kierney said. "You know we have different sentiments on... the physical existence of evil... how it manifests itself, in this country or elsewhere. Perhaps it is a generational thing. I believed I made that clear on the day I agreed to replace..."

"They follow me," the old voice hissed from behind him, like judgment.

"Who does? Who? The Macoute?"

A nod.

"How do you know?"

"The flowers..."

"*The flowers were evidence of nothing,*" Fr. Kierney cut him off once again. This time he felt the anger and he heard it as well: He had spoken truly. "Since I've been here we've been shouted at, stones flung at our cars, locals we even befriend beaten with sticks. We've been spit on by passers-by, stolen from, threatened almost weekly. Almost daily. That's life in an unstable political environment; it isn't the first time I've had to live through this. I've been in Central America. I've been in Brazil. Why do you think the Macoute is out to get you today any more than they were yesterday? Or the day before?"

The old priest was watching him, stern now, those intense, brooding features filled like the fullness of a cloud.

"Be assured, vain man," he said quietly, and his wide four fingers tapped the syllables on Fr. Kierney's table.

"What is this? More prophecy?"

"Be assured," the older man rumbled, like a boiler muttering under its top. *"That your sin will find you out."*

▢ ▢ ▢

That night Fr. Kierney dreamed. In the dream he was taking communion from a senior priest, a figure who was at times Maretin and at times a figure whose face was shaded and could not be seen. The communion wafer hovered close to his lips and as he inclined his head to receive it the bread was drawn away from him, drawn back and replaced on the golden smooth plate as unworthy to be received. Again the mysterious hand would lower the bread, again the inclination of the mouth, the readying heart; drawn away. Then he saw the face that was hidden in a cowl and it was changing, grinning with a terrible mirth, the old and stiffened flesh of Fr. Maretin growing outward around the mouth into the sloping bone and narrow slit-eyes of a goat.

He awoke in his cot and someone was near his door: The swing curtain swayed just slightly in the tropical no-wind that was nighttime. The shadow that was part only of greater shadow, only distinguished by being a lesser dark than its surroundings, moved on, and Fr. Kierney lying back in his bed of sweat heard a thin, metallic sound, something bonging like a faint bell off down the hallway. He slept again.

▢ ▢ ▢

When next he awoke it was to the sharp clap-thunder of automatic gunfire. "Get out, get up and take only what you need to wear and get out of here," the scared, bright face of one of the orderlies was shouting at him. "Father. Are you awake?"

The compound was a crazy hive of people running. Medicals were blockading the doors to the infirmary and simultaneously rolling all delicate equipment on casters toward the back rooms. There were people trying to get local volunteers and lab assistants and food-liners out the side doors, even out windows. Again came the sound of gunfire, the sharp stinging blow in the ear.

"It's a Macoute raid," the bright scared face said to him. "They're shooting people out front. Out front."

The orderly gestured crazily toward the front gates as if Fr. Kierney might not have known where they were; then he was gone in the race. Someone knocked over a glass case full of ampoules, the whole collection sundering on the tile floor with a liquid hiss. He grabbed the arm of the woman leaning down to sweep them up.

"Toxic?" he said quick. "Poison?"

"Mwen pa konnen." Her expression was vivid and scared.

"Leave it," he said, pulling off the jacket he had hastily grabbed and dropping it over the spill. "Just get out. The back way."

He pushed through to the front gates, stopped at the door when another violent rattle shook the air, making someone shriek. He looked outside, the sleep still rolling under his eyes.

It was nearly dawn, the light a level gray vacillating between periods of night still hovering over the hills. There was a cool wetness in the air, the last blush of cool before explosive morning; he could still see stars. Two Macoute men had a Haitian man in a white doctor's coat down on his knees in the dirt. The other Macoutes smiled from behind mirrored glasses, some of them wearing the tilted black berets that were emblematic of the army as well. Three or four jeeps had been pulled up onto compound grounds and their headlights criss-crossed into a rough circle of electric light where the man knelt. One Macoute officer was slapping the man lightly back and forth, from one cheek to the other, with a pistol.

Many hands grabbed at him as he came through the door, someone wedging him back into shadow.

"Don't," the voice said in English. "Stay right here. Don't interfere. This isn't a black-on-white thing. They only want their own."

Someone tried to bolt from the circle of Macoutes and was brought back, kicking against the forms of two men who pinned him to the ground. The one who had tried to run was light-skinned, possibly not even a native. When he started to struggle again the Macoute with the pistol stepped over and shot him through the head.

"No, Jesus, oh no, Jesus no..." Fr. Kierney heard himself saying, but the hands from the building's side held him faster.

"You want to make more dead?" another voice said, close in his ear like a lover. "You step out there and they'll start shooting us all. You want more like him? Let it be."

The other Macoute men cheered the shot and gave an enthusiastic blast of automatic shells upward into the indifferent air. The one who had not done the shooting grinned wide and waved his hands in enjoyment of the applause, but the one with the pistol had no expression at all. He returned toward the kneeling man and started slapping him on the cheeks with the pistol end again.

"Don't try it, don't try," the voice said, and Fr. Kierney realized he had been moving forward. "Look at us. We're twenty hiding here. Twenty to two or three. Those men owed money to Uncle Sack. That's all. That's all."

The kneeling man raised his head up as if to say something

and for a moment the two Macoute listened; then the happy one pointed a finger at the kneeling man and mimed shooting him.

"*Boka! Boka!*" he cried, turning to the others for applause. When he didn't receive any he looked angry. He took the pistol from the other one's hand and shot the kneeling man in the mouth. The kneeling man had continued to talk up until the end.

"*Boka! Boka!*" he cried to the group, and this time the others cheered. The first Macoute had still no expression on his face and stood examining the bodies in the dust at his feet as if they might have something else to show him. Then for the first time he looked up and for a moment Fr. Kierney believed the killer was staring directly at him. The man smiled, a peaceful, almost naive happiness. He gestured over their heads.

The other Macoutes started laughing too, one of them throwing a bottle that skidded in the direction of Fr. Kierney and the hiding others. But it was over their heads they were pointing, where the first live cinders were beginning to rise from the roof of the mission house, the two connected buildings behind them where a strange light was walking the halls and spreading itself like a presence born of the air.

"My God, my dear God," Fr. Kierney said, and this time he was free, running out into the lighter part of the grounds and his head spinning around as if to catch all the damage that was taking place at once, as if to hold some of it back. The main entrance house caught so quickly that level sheets of flame had already started running across the walkway scaffolding toward the greenhouse. From the other end of the compound the roof of the infirmary area was starting to leak a brilliant light from six and then ten and then a dozen fissures. Another small cloud of cinders scattered across the lot, bringing this time the rich smell of gasoline.

"There's no one inside to stop it, there's no..."

Fr. Kierney halted when he saw the Macoute men looking at

him. The face of the first one had returned to its expressionless state, as blank as the look of a zombi under the winking sunglasses. He stared at Fr. Kierney in the manner of someone staring at an object, something that might be out of place. Then the laughing one slapped him on the back and climbed in his jeep. After a minute the expressionless Macoute joined him and the small group circled once around the *blan* priest, their jeep engines gunning loud, before pulling out into the dawn-colored fields and away.

People were running back and forth around the flaming buildings now, some emerging from doors carrying boxes and supplies, one man Fr. Kierney had never seen before hauling a suitcase full of clothes. There was a soft crackling as something came down through an interior ceiling and black smoke began spreading out through the air as if it had all been miraculously contained until just that moment. The same orderly with a handkerchief around his mouth now ran up to Fr. Kierney and pushed him so hard the priest sat down stiffly on the ground.

"Get away! Get away!" the orderly shouted. "You're too close!" He stooped to take Fr. Kierney's arm.

"They'll never find him," Fr. Kierney said.

"Get back! Father, please!"

"They'll never find him! They'll never..." Fr. Kierney cried, but the half-concealed face of the orderly did not understand him, and above and behind that shining face Fr. Kierney was struck by the sudden beauty of a galaxy of flame-bearing cinders making their way up and across the dawn sky, replacing each of the vanishing stars one after one in their same assigned locations.

Epilogue
In the City of Sleeping Houses

Thomas LeFay looked south where three lean, graceless pelicans descended in unbroken horizontal paths toward a surface of water that they did not reach, the front one and then the
others kicking webby feet down into the evening tide and then
convulsing their brown, controlled bodies in that way a sail has
when caught in wind, motionless now as they moved up and across
the minutely-changing horizon. By mountain standards it would
have been already twilight, but day here waited low against the
earth before giving way and LeFay knew that what was called
"evening" would run on without definite edges, like brass in a
smelter. The color of shadows along the visible roots and verandas
in all the front yards as he walked past them drifted from gray to
storm blue to purple, and still evening was there; and LeFay, having had a drink at an outside bar and walked a bit around the
gaudy tourist places and seen the cats still mellowing in the sun,
came back to the same spot and watched it just starting to become
evening all over again. A woman walked up to his side.

"*Würden Sie?*" she said, holding out the camera.

"*Für dich,* anything," LeFay smiled, and her three friends
laughed in unison. Smooth, clean-lined bodies in breeze-billowed
cotton. He snapped them next to the NINETY MILES TO CUBA

marker and handed the camera back over, his mind passing away from the grim happy faces even before his own face had ceased obliging them with return smiles. They were gone.

Do you love me? Do you?

In the background of his thoughts the sound of the pier sellers continued on, louder now that the third or fourth false evening was nearing its close and the off-season buyers would soon be taking their pink lotioned forms shadowlike into other parts of town: to Mallory Square, where a man played "Amazing Grace" on a bagpipe and another man, surely, drew wallets out of back pockets with the deftness of a trained artist; to the formal estates where kings and presidents had slept and made war; to the unused lighthouse that stood like a sentinel over this town embraced by the sea. The pier sellers behind him cried the virtues of conch, tiny Jamaican flags, shot glasses, carved floatwood, their chatter drifting in his ears.

"Oh, hell," LeFay said, aloud but to himself when the drink refused to do to him what he had hoped it might. "All right. If it's going to be that way, all right."

The walk to the east side was long and he had several chances to change his mind, all of which he took, but he remained walking. Overpriced, flamingo-colored bed and breakfasts with names like *Eden House* and *Lorelei* merged with stucco-fronted churches and double-decker porches virtually lost among the foliage. *I'm only going across town,* he assured himself, not aloud this time as this was in the area of private beaches, the expensive part of the Key where the stern muffled aura of a church always seemed to pervade the air. *I'm walking around town because I haven't been here in a while and it's a good idea to work off that drink before I try and drive north again. That's why and that's it,* and then he was lost for a moment outside a laundromat where three men in gray unsmoothable clothes and tee-shirts watched him pass, their worlds rotating dully behind glass ports. LeFay considered briefly the possibility that he might get beaten up for walking belligerently through the wrong part of town at the wrong time, and what a wincingly delicious irony that would be; then passed the thought over. If it would be it would be and it probably would not be. The three-columned French baroque grillwork gave way to cigar and shotgun houses, their walls a somnolent yellow and peeling, the broad hanging branches of a banyan tree sawed away to allow passage where it broke from the sidewalk and heaved the bricks partly up.

God but this is a beautiful place, LeFay thought, and through his sudden emotion realized the drink must actually have hit him more than he realized. He walked side by side with the rest of the thought, neither accepting nor rejecting it, feeling the day-heat still lingering in the cracked asphalt and opening up his pores: *she would have liked it here.* Then he found his way again and was passing the cemetery.

He pressed between two halves of a lockless gate and stepped into the graveyard, the what-looked-like miles of scrollwork graves and names, the dates, the pieces of time reserved, unread. The Jewish people sectioned carefully off with a fence lest anyone think, LeFay thought, that they died silent and unrequited like the rest of us; cemetery earth so broad and sweeping that markers had been erected at the corners like street signs to help you navigate your way. For some time, it seemed, his feet merely crunched through the gravel pathways that led in all directions to more mausoleums and limestone carving. Then he came to the far east corner and left the cemetery for streetside and the mnemonic he had heard once and had not even known he had committed to memory worked: her house was there.

At the front door a girl in a sundress greeted him. She looked neither Haitian nor Cuban, but was perhaps Cuban; LeFay watched her turn and walk simply back into the recesses of the foyer which was like a treasure-trove of tinkling artifacts. Her hair in back was exceedingly long and straight and had been knotted several times down its length. He stepped inside and took a chair underneath the enormous shellacked body of a sea turtle, from whose bottom feet descended chimes made of glass. On a rough mantelpiece stood at least fifteen icons of the Blessed Virgin, looking down in bland indifference at the written requests tucked underneath their serpent-wrapped feet. An old black man who had been sitting in one of the three empty chairs looked LeFay over well without discomfort or hiding and stood, having made some decision, and made his way back out the front door. LeFay watched him negotiate the screen and the porch with its twin stone angels flanking the steps and then he was alone. The girl returned.

"The *mambo* is not well," she said. "She says come back another time."

"Tell her I've been to St. Marc," LeFay said, instinctively reaching for American money in one hand and discarding it as instinctively as useless. "Tell her I know *Père* Maretin and Henri Santil and Ginee LeClair. Tell her I know about her. Tell her that."

"She is not well," the girl said uncertainly, but she went into the back room and in a minute the flower-spotted curtain was opened by an unseen string somewhere and LeFay went in.

The *mambo's* own chamber was filled with copper-colored wire cages hung from every corner and from various tall pieces of wood that had been propped on their ends. Inside the cages green and sky-blue macaws chortled in their throats, their strange pow-der-white feet opening and closing on perches and their head crests opening out into shuttering plumes. There was a strong smell of the birds and a sense of them, live and quick, stepping around their confined spaces from all sides. LeFay ducked underneath a cage from which a lesser one hung by wire and came in amid a dry flutter, having to look around for a minute in the sheeted gloom before he saw her at the far end of the room.

The *mambo* was seated by a window and the age was on her face in a way he had not expected to see. Thick, trenchant marks fell from underneath the broadly-spread eyes and suggested the contours of bone underneath with a frankness that was almost an exposure, gathering again at the rims of her mouth and then descending into the softness under her chin. The skin itself was sinking into obscurity around her eyes and mouth, not of dirt or uncleanness, but the color of deepening waters. He sat in the only available chair.

"Henri," the *mambo* said, those deeply-set eyes peering out the window where the southern horizon was visible, just detectable between a stand of battered houses. "Is my chick still alive?"

"He's alive," LeFay said. "So are many others. They say it's thanks to you. You send them good *djok.*"

"And the Baron? He lives?"

"Oui," he said. *"Et aussi Baron Samedi."*

The *mambo* laughed.

"This is America, *non?"* she said, looking now at him and the laugh betraying something behind it that did not laugh, perhaps never had. "We can speak English. The Baron never dies."

"There is unrest," LeFay said. "There is a lot of unrest in the people. The people are ready to become organized, if someone..."

"The people," the *mambo* said, and her intonation made LeFay stop. There was a silence, only troubled by the stiff-paper sound of macaw wings.

"Père Aristide is making headlines all through the presses," he tried again. "Even here in America. Even in France. They can't

kill him now, not any more. If they wanted to, if they wanted to kill him or disappear him, they've missed their chance. He's daily news."

The *mambo* peered out the window again. Where the sun met her forehead a broad plane of near-skull showed brightly, the colored headpiece she wore tied into her hair already gone into the nighttime gloaming. *But it isn't night yet,* LeFay thought, and wondered why the previous distinction seemed so important to him at that moment.

"The Baron never dies," the *mambo* said.

"If the newspapers run my work..."

"The Baron never dies."

"All right. If that's the way it is, I suppose to you that's the way it's always going to be. That's all right," LeFay said, angry somehow without being able to trace the anger. "What I want from you is to know about a woman. A white woman."

The *mambo* looked across at him then, quizzically.

"You want Mamma Loa to spot out a *blan* woman for you?" She started to laugh, the face etched with new lines. "You want Mamma to use the Eye? To use the Eye to look all the way *lòt bò dlo?*"

"She lived at the mission in St. Marc until the Macoute burned it down. The last word I got was she had escaped the fire and was staying with a family of Catholics named DeTroyen. They have a house in the north, near Cap..."

But the *mambo* laughed. "Ain't no whites in *Ayiti, mon cher,*" she said, her bracelets clacking on wrists LeFay could have wrapped two fingers around. "Ain't no such thing, *pas du tout.* Never was." She grinned toothfully at him, whispered. *"And even they don't know it."*

The old woman rocked noiselessly until a coughing took her, and then LeFay gritted himself and watched her withered chest which seemed to be almost hollow behind the cage of bones. The sound was bad; too deep, too long.

"Better you don't come back, *blan*," the *mambo* said, bundling herself like a cold person in the room where the air was dust and the smell of macaws and LeFay thought must have topped eighty degrees under the elaborate shades. "What this Mamma has, it ain't for white use. Not any more."

She settled back in her chair, looking uninterestedly at the floor.

LeFay rose to go. "What do I owe you?" he said.

"Blue eyes," the *mambo* laughed to herself, quietly. "A couple a' pretty blue eyes."

□   □   □

Outside the house LeFay walked directly into low sun and let it flash into him with the crossing of every branch overhead, not stopping to flinch or prevent the mounting spots that blinded his walking little by little. In a farther part of the neighborhood he passed a playground where kids were banging the side of a hollow trash can with a metal bar, the gonging-clashing coming straight into his head with the flashes of sun, a pain and a distraction. On the whitened perch of a tombstone a large gray pelican suddenly alighted, shaking its wings once and arranging its long obsidian gaze at him.

Quincunx. Last night I dreamed of a tree sprouting from the navel of a corpse.

Then it was abruptly truly sunset and he had only gotten halfway back through the cemetery, and he stopped and saw the light finally shift over, the heat seemingly dispersing in an instant. He thought of the odor of kerosene being applied now to jump-hoops by someone out on the pier, fireworks leaping in one quick desperate frenzy over the water. He thought of the sight of the day boats coming in close to see the performers: the magician and the small-stunts acrobat, and the card-reader, and the palm-reader, and the tourists losing money to all these people but doing it because they knew they were at home no matter where they went, no matter what edge of the country they stood in they were *there,* in that belonging place, carrying the place with them under their feet and having it always as part of their standing. LeFay's head ached. The trees filled in with gloom and then a sudden, new darkness and there was a sound: From nearby he heard a small swelling, a tremulousness in the air where there had been no sound before:

It's the birds, LeFay thought, turning his head into the nothing here and there to see them, to see the trees suddenly alive and crazed with them, who would be emerging in a wild and unbroken stream; but it was not; and when instead he came and put himself close to the wall of one of the mausoleums, its sides now moon-colored and hovering in the cemetery grass, he knew what the noise was. The walls were full of bees, nested thick within all four corners, their number building in a low mounting howl sharp and alive and rising into the emergent night like a birth-cry from the houses of the dead.

William Orem is a Maryland native living in Bloomington, Indiana, where he is completing a dissertation on the works of James Joyce and John Cage. His short stories, poetry and journalism have appeared in numerous small presses, including AQR, Sou'wester and Exquisite Corpse. He is currently at work on his second novel.

LAUREN PROLL